THE SCARECROW MURDERS

MILLIE RAVENSWORTH

Copyright © 2023 by Millie Ravensworth

All rights reserved.

No part of this book may be reproduced in any form or by any electronic or mechanical means, including information storage and retrieval systems, without written permission from the author, except for the use of brief quotations in a book review.

1

Penny was up early, driven from her bed by the August sunshine streaming through her bedroom windows and the gentle but incessant whines of a young dog who wanted his breakfast. Penny looked at the little corgi.

"Maybe I should train you to get your own breakfast, Monty. And make mine while you're at it. You're probably clever enough."

In the early spring, Monty had played a small part in uncovering a hunk of buried golden treasure, and only two weeks ago had found a small sack full of bank notes which, as far as Penny was aware, anyone had yet to claim from the police station. In the eyes of some locals, Monty was a treasure-hunting super-dog. But could he make his own breakfast? Of course not.

As Penny went downstairs to the shop, she could tell it was going to be a very warm day. The Cozy Craft sewing shop was an old building, which stayed cooler than most, but Penny still carried out the physical chores in the early morning, knowing she might not have the energy later on when things got hotter.

By the time her cousin Izzy arrived at work, Penny had almost finished rearranging the window display with some of the ideas they wanted to showcase for the upcoming scarecrow festival.

Many towns and villages had scarecrow festivals in the late summer and early autumn, but the committee this year had decided to give Framlingham's festival an extra zing by holding it in the inner grounds of Framlingham castle. Framlingham was a small and bustling market town, one of many small and bustling market towns in Suffolk, but none of the others had a twelfth century castle on the hill. Holding the festival inside the castle walls would add an extra sense of occasion, and maybe help the committee raise even more money for the Community Change charity.

"Scarecrow fun!" Izzy chanted as she paused to admire the display.

"I hope it will be," said Penny.

"It's going to bring out everyone's creativity," said Izzy and presented Penny with a chocolate sprinkled coffee from the café along the road.

To encourage the creativity of scarecrow builders in the area, Izzy had developed a face kit for those who wanted to customise the features of their scarecrow and had even recorded a video showing how to put them together. They had patterns for hats and costumes, and some fun gingham fabrics that complemented the country aesthetic.

"I can't wait to see all the different scarecrows people come up with."

They had set up a demonstration table outside on the pavement, with a bale of straw next to it. It seemed like a good investment to draw in people who hadn't started on their own scarecrow yet. They didn't have long, though. The castle was receiving contributions until Friday so they could set up for the launch event on Sunday.

The bell above the door rang, signalling the arrival of their first customers. As the morning wore on and more scarecrow making customers turned up, Penny found herself getting caught up in the excitement of the festival. She and Izzy helped a group of children who wanted to make a *Stranger Things* scarecrow wearing a baseball cap like the character Dustin. They ended up assembling their creation on the table outside. Penny watched as the group worked together, laughing and chatting as they stuffed the scarecrow's clothes with straw. She couldn't help but smile at their enthusiasm. It was contagious. Monty was very happy to stroll in and out of the doorway, reminding everybody that he was available for fuss and attention.

Denise Upton, one of the local GPs, came into the shop to chat to them.

"Good morning, ladies," she said. "I need to get started on my scarecrow, or so everyone has been telling me. Apparently, if I don't make one, I will be ostracised from the community. And I gather this is the ideal place to start."

"It is," said Izzy. "And what kind of scarecrow is it going to be?"

"The kind that stands in a field with a straw hat on its head?"

"Most people tend to go for a theme."

"Ah, then perhaps I could make it a surgeon scarecrow, complete with stethoscope and lab coat. I've got some bits and bobs lying about. What do you think?"

"Great idea," said Penny. "You've got the lab coat. We have some fabric that would be perfect for crafting the other parts you'll need. We've been using unbleached calico for making hands and faces, which is just right for a scarecrow, and it's easy to add features if you want to."

"I'm not great at sewing," said Denise.

"You're a doctor," said Penny.

"Oh, I can probably stitch up wounds well enough, but I'm not saying my stitching is neat or even."

"I'll bear that in mind. Or, if you don't want to do sewing, there's an old-school option if you want. Ask Izzy about that crate under the table."

"Tell me about the crate under table please, Izzy," said Denise, playing along.

"Mangelwurzels," said Izzy.

"Bless you!" said Denise. She pulled one out. "Is this a kind of vegetable?"

"Yes. Mangelwurzels are used for animal feed, but we got a crate of them cheap for kids to use as heads," said Izzy.

"Plus Izzy likes saying 'mangelwurzel'," called Penny, who had retreated further into the shop.

"It's true. Mangelwurzel," said Izzy. "Now, in terms of your scarecrow, what's the funniest accessory a surgeon can have?"

"Hm. Funny like scrubs caps that slide over your eyes because they are all men-sized?" asked Denise, pulling a face. "Because let me tell you, that's no joke."

"Perhaps something more obviously ridiculous, like a kidney in a bucket. You should make a pile of kidneys out of felt."

Denise peered at Izzy. "I think you're mixing up surgeons with pathologists, or maybe even butchers."

"Nope. You know I'm right. Go with something funny and gross, the kids will love it."

The bell rang again and Aubrey Jones stepped inside. Aubrey, local painter, decorator and all round handyman, was one of the first people to show a friendly face to Penny when she moved to Framlingham. She'd even thought there might be something more than friendship between them, but that was before Denise took advantage of Penny's dithering and swooped in to take him for herself. Still, he remained one of the most cheery and likeable people Penny met around the town. Today however, he had an uncharacteristically thunderous look on his face. His greeting was a loud huff.

"Honey, what's wrong?" said Denise, putting a hand on his paint-dotted overalls.

"Some people!" Aubrey huffed again but added nothing more.

"I sense it has something to do with people," said Izzy.

Aubrey gave a third huff, for all the good it was doing him, and waved a hand violently in a non-specific direction. "That woman up at Pageant House. Eve Bennefer. Just sent me away with a flea in my ear!"

"Oh?"

"I just went up there to finish up the painting in the kitchen and she starts yelling at me – well, not yelling, maybe – but getting shirty about the fact it wasn't convenient for me to be there and I should clear off."

"Some people can be so rude," said Denise, stroking his chest.

"Can't say I know her," said Penny.

Aubrey put his hand on Denise's as a seeming act of affection, but Penny could tell it was to stop her chest stroking motions.

"She's only just bought the place," he said. "Contracted me to paint it all, top to bottom. Been doing a good job an' all while she was away. And that's not easy, squeezing it in between jobs for his nibs and helping out with the bunting at the castle for the scarecrow festival." He glanced at his watch.

"Well, if Mrs Bennefer doesn't want you…" said Denise in a coy voice.

"You're right. Off to the castle, then," he said, which probably wasn't what Denise had been hinting at. "That bunting won't hang itself." He gave Denise a peck on the cheek and with a "Penny, Izzy," for the shop owners, headed to the door, where he paused. "Speaking of his nibs," he said and nodded through the window.

'His nibs' was Stuart Dinktrout, garden centre owner, pig fancier, chair of the local chamber of commerce and general all-round middle-aged busybody; that certain type of man who seemed to think that just because he had silvery hair and a deep, cultured voice, he should be listened to and fawned over every time he spoke.

As Aubrey left and Izzy rang up the materials Denise was purchasing, Stuart Dinktrout remained outside, clearly hovering in some unhappy manner. When Denise departed, Penny followed her out onto the pavement. Better to see what Stuart wanted, rather than have him hanging around like some mood-sucking misery.

2

"Hello, Stuart," Penny said cheerily.

Penny found that being cheery to grumpy people helped. Sometimes it lifted their mood, sometimes it annoyed them further and popped their grump bubble so they'd actually reveal what was bothering them.

Stuart Dinktrout scowled at her. "Do you have a permit?"

"A fishing permit?" she suggested.

Izzy came out to join her.

"You need a permit in order to have that table outside," he said, gesturing at their scarecrow station on the pavement. "You may not put street furniture in place without a permit from the town council. We take public safety very seriously, and of course the access needs of the disabled are always a priority."

Penny knew very well that having the final word on any tiny point of order was Stuart's *actual* personal priority, but as chair of the chamber of commerce, he could not be ignored, so she kept that thought to herself.

"Sorry, Stuart. We weren't aware."

"Oblivious," agreed Izzy.

"Could we apply for one in retrospect, do you think? We really want to support the Scarecrow Festival, and we know how important it is for the chamber of commerce. It's your name on the banners, right?"

Penny saw that Stuart was conflicted. On the one hand he wanted to have the moral high ground, but on the other, he wanted the scarecrow festival to succeed.

"I suppose if you fill in the form I can see that it's fast-tracked through the process."

"Oh, that sounds like a solution," said Penny sweetly.

"And, er, what other things can we do if we have a permit?" asked Izzy.

Stuart looked at her suspiciously. "It depends what you ask for. Selling food and drink might be permitted, outside a restaurant of course. Advertising stands are a common request."

Penny thought that Stuart detected the gleam in Izzy's eye.

He coughed hurriedly. "My advice to you would be to keep it simple in the first instance, so you are better positioned to be granted permission. You can apply for an extension afterwards if you so desire."

"Always nice to have your help," said Penny. "I'm sure you have other shops to inspect. Perhaps preparations at the castle for the festival on Sunday."

She was dismissing him. She could tell he knew she was

dismissing him. His business with them was done, and he probably did have important things to attend to elsewhere, but the thought of him, Stuart Dinktrout, being dismissed by this young outsider made him bristle. He did a funny little twitch, turned on his heel, and marched off.

"Permits, eh?" said Izzy as they went back in.

"How will little Fram cope without some pointless bureaucracy and self-important middle-class curtain twitchers?"

The door jangled behind them. Penny looked round. She gave a heartfelt sigh when she saw who it was.

"Hello, Carmella," said Izzy. "We were just talking about you."

Carmella Mountjoy owned the Wickham Dress Agency in the next town over. It was a very different shop to Cozy Craft, but Carmella had convinced herself that they were rivals. Carmella was slender and statuesque, always stylishly dressed, and she would be a stunningly beautiful middle-aged woman – if she didn't have a permanent expression like a dog chewing a stinging nettle.

"I see you're cashing in on the scarecrow thing," said Carmella with a wave at the table out on the pavement.

"If you mean we're helping the town become involved in the festival to raise money for Community Change, then yes."

"I think they're hoping to buy a new minibus for the old folks and the scouts," said Izzy.

"It seemed like the public-spirited thing to do," said Penny.

"Shame you don't have anything like this in Wickham

Market," said Izzy, "or you could have made a scarecrow yourself."

"Oh it doesn't matter that I don't live here," said Carmella. "I checked the rules and anyone may enter a scarecrow."

"Oh, so you're going to enter?" asked Penny.

"As if I would share my plans with you," said Carmella.

"Oh, yes. Plans must be kept secret," said Izzy conspiratorially and put a finger to her lips.

Carmella failed to spot the sarcasm. She made a show of looking around the shop. "Where is it then? Where's your entry?"

"Is that why you're here? To scope out the competition?" Penny laughed. "We haven't started yet."

"I don't know if we're even entering," said Izzy. "Busy, busy, busy."

Carmella harumphed. "Of course you will. You like making likenesses of people."

"Do we?"

"I know you two made a likeness of me. You'll have it shut away, of course."

"Likenesses of you? Is this that voodoo doll thing again?"

"Yes!" hissed Carmella. "You admit it!"

"I admit we made a teddy bear – a teddy bear! – that you thought was a voodoo doll," said Penny.

"My shoulder has been so painful in recent weeks and there is no medical explanation. I have been examined by the finest doctors of Harley Street and they have found *nothing*. That means it can *only* be you two. Admit it, you've made effigies and stuck pins in them!"

"Is that seriously the best explanation you can come up

with?" asked Penny. "We've discussed this before Carmella, and the situation remains the same. We are not obsessed with you. We do not make effigies of you, and we definitely do not stick pins in them."

"Aha! Stick pins in *what*? You just incriminated yourself with your poor sentence structure!" She waggled her skinny arms in triumph.

"Go away, Carmella. Please. It's too sunny a day for arguments. We are very busy and we don't have time for your nonsense today." Penny flapped the length of viscose that she was folding at Carmella. It wafted gently, which wasn't quite the dramatic effect she'd have liked.

"I'm not done with you!" Carmella snapped and flounced from the shop. As she passed the table outside, she batted aside the scarecrow construction broomsticks which stood in a large box and sent them clattering across the pavement in her wake.

Monty barked at Carmella now that she was safely at a distance.

"Is she more nutso than usual?" said Izzy.

"It's the summer heat," said Penny and they went out together to collect the sticks and put them back in their box.

"I do hope Dr Denise does make a bucket of felt kidneys to go with her scarecrow," said Izzy. "I think that would look good."

"She does like to throw herself into community life, which can't be easy with a busy job like hers."

Izzy made a small, amused noise.

"What?" said Penny.

"Nothing. Just impressed how nice you remain to her, even though she done you wrong and stole your man."

"What is this? A country and western song?"

"I'm just saying…"

"Uh-huh. You saying I need to get back on the horse and find me a new man perhaps?"

Izzy looked thoughtful. "I'd love to have a horse."

Penny laughed. "You have a boyfriend, several dogs, sheep on the way, did I hear? You do not need any other large mammals in your life."

"Thank you for calling my boyfriend a large mammal," Izzy grinned.

"Sorry, I didn't mean to—"

"I mean technically he is. He's—"

"*Please* do not finish that sentence," Penny cut in. "I do not wish to know. My, my. It's getting warm, isn't it? Maybe one of us should go and get some ice creams. Lickety Splits should be open by now."

"Always happy to help. With ice creams," said Izzy and left Penny to it while she wandered up towards ice cream parlour near the castle.

3

The burning sun of midday gave way to a softer but still baking heat in the late afternoon.

"Walk time, Monty," said Penny. "Can't put it off any longer."

Monty looked up from his basket, tongue lolling.

"You've not been out all day. Let's make it a decent walk, eh?"

Izzy brought in some of the disparate oddments left over from the scarecrow table. "I'll finish up with these and then shut up for the afternoon. I've got a Frambeat Gazette meeting."

"On a Monday?"

"Glenmore wants the scarecrow festival edition to be something extra special. Also, they have air conditioning in the residents lounge."

Hot pavements were painful to doggy paw pads, so Penny carried Monty down Market Hill, diverting around the bin bags of donations someone had thoughtlessly dumped in front of the charity shop. She cut through behind the Elms flats to Framlingham Mere, where Monty could run around on cool mud to his heart's content. Framlingham Mere was a large and unusual stretch of land sitting directly beneath the castle. For parts of the year the whole place was a lake, while in warmer months it was just a pond with wide marshy edges. The waters shifted with the seasons, and a small herd of cows grazed wherever they could roam. Penny had read that, in the Middle Ages, the mere had provided the castle with fish.

The area was picturesque and very much loved by wildlife. Penny led Monty to the lush green rushes at the edge of the wettest parts. Everywhere was alive with the sounds of birds, although most of them disappeared at Monty's approach. A beautiful willow tree leaned at an impossible angle over the water, fronds of leaves hanging down in a curtain. If Penny looked up she could see the castle wall above them. It was a lovely tranquil place. Penny inhaled deeply, feeling that she was feeding her body and soul with the beauty and peace of it all.

"No, no, no! Seriously, dogs are the worst!"

Penny heard the voice, but could not locate its source. Monty had no such difficulty and launched himself into the greenery with a tiny yip of enthusiasm.

A whole person rose up out of the rushes, unfurling like a weird fern.

"Your little dog has chased away every bird in this area," complained the tall young man. He wore camouflage clothing and had a strange canopy draped over his head and a camera with a huge zoom lens hanging from his neck. He stomped onto the path, and put down a small folding stool, which he had been sitting on.

"Sorry?" Penny said. She didn't want to apologise, because she had done nothing wrong, but she also didn't understand what was happening; so she fell back on the English term used instead of "Please explain yourself" in peculiar social situations. However, this man was clearly not English – he spoke the language too well, too precisely – and he had taken the word as an apology.

"I should think you are," he said. "I have missed my chance now."

"You have missed what chance exactly?" Penny asked. "And what are you doing lurking in the undergrowth?"

"Lurking?" he said, his annoyance giving way to a flicker of amusement.

"Lurking," she repeated.

He sighed, as though expelling the last of his irritation. "There have been rumours of a white-tailed lapwing here. I'm sure I don't need to explain what a big deal that is."

Penny hesitated. "You might want to. A little. A lapwing is a bird, right?"

The man tutted. "How do you not know this?" He produced a sketchbook, flicked through the pages and showed her a deftly drawn sketch of a small wading bird. "Yes, it is a bird that is very rare to see here in England. It would be such a triumph if I might spot it here, and capture a photograph." He held up the expensive looking camera. There was a passionate zeal, a wonderful energy in his eyes when he spoke on what was clearly an important topic for him. "However, with your little dog scaring off all of the birds it is not at all likely."

Monty barked, happy to be part of the conversation.

"Look, I am sorry about that," said Penny. "But I am sure I'm not the first dog walker to disturb you, and I won't be the last. It's a public footpath, after all."

"I don't expect you to understand. I have been here all day. *De morgenstond heeft goud in de mond*, you know?"

"The morning is, er...?"

"You say the bird in the morning eats worms."

"The early bird catches the worm?"

"Indeed! All day I have been here. When I think I have a sighting, I must crouch down in the best place to hide, and it's not always somewhere convenient. I need time to put up my portable hide."

He dragged the canopy out of the bushes, and Penny saw some of the difficulty. "Do you put this up every time? That must disturb the birds more than any dog."

"Too true!"

It reminded Penny of the toilet tents she had seen on campsites. A small cubicle that could be placed around a ... seated person. She didn't imagine they were complicated things to put up, but erecting a tent was never a silent process.

"Is this really the best way to hide yourself from the birds?" she asked. She peered at a corner of the tent shell. It was some sort of nylon fabric, printed with a camouflage design.

He pursed his lips as he tugged the rest of the canopy out onto the path. "I bought it from the internet for this trip. It promised discreet and quick concealment, but it has not performed well. I came to England, where many birds can be seen, but this has been a disappointment." He gave another heartfelt sigh at this point.

"Well I am sorry that we hasn't lived up to your expectations," said Penny. "Especially if it's important for your trip. You've come all the way from... Where have you come from?"

"Belgium. I am Remi de Smet. I am staying at the College Road holiday lodges."

"Nice to meet you, Remi. I am Penny. So you came all the way from Belgium and this piece of equipment is letting you down."

He shrugged in mild defeat, all of the complaining gone from him now. "I have another week after this one, but these are specialist items and I cannot get anything else at this point."

Penny looked at the bizarre structure. "You know, I can't make any promises at all, but if you wanted to call into the Cozy Craft shop in the town, it's possible we can help you to adapt it, or replace it with something better suiting your needs."

"Cozy Craft?"

"We do sewing. We make dresses. But we can turn our hand to many things."

"Cozy Craft?"

"That's the one."

He looked extremely sceptical, but gave a shrug. "Maybe I will do that."

4

The Frambeat Gazette was a free local paper, operated entirely by volunteers, and their meetings took place in the conveniently placed lounge of Miller Fields sheltered accommodation, where its elderly editor in chief, Glenmore Wilson, happened to live. The air con was on, but it did little to bring the temperature down. There was also a noisy electric fan plugged in nearby, stirring up the muggy air of the lounge. The flow of air was directed at Glenmore, probably because he set it up. Izzy shunted her chair over so that she could get a little whiffle of breeze.

Glenmore held down the papers in front of him with his one good hand to stop the fan blowing them away. "The upcoming scarecrow festival presents an opportunity for a souvenir edition of the paper."

"Seems like nearly every other edition we put out is a souvenir edition," said Annalise, the local librarian.

"And so they should be," said Glenmore. "I know there are local residents who are proud of their collection of Frambeat Gazettes. But this should be an extra special souvenir edition."

"Extra special," Izzy noted.

"With lots of extra photographs," said Glenmore. "Tariq, you will take care of that, I assume?"

Tariq, who had initially joined the Frambeat Gazette team as part of his university placement, was the Gazette's never-ending source of youthful vigour and burning ambition. He pursued every story as if it could win him a prestigious journalism award, wilfully ignoring the fact that it was a small local paper, rarely featuring bigger issues than who won what prize for which jam at the local Women's Institute.

"I certainly will. I have some new photographic equipment and I can't wait to put it to the test."

"New equipment?"

Tariq reached down to the floor and lifted up a large box with a sleek black drone on the front. "Aerial photography!" he said, thrilled.

"We expecting many scarecrows in the air?" said Glenmore drily. He had been a military man in his earlier life, a life that had cost him his arm (although Izzy had never built up the courage to ask him the details) and Glenmore was very hard to surprise or impress.

"Shots of the castle and the scarecrows from the air will look very professional," said Tariq. "In fact, I'm going to get up there and shoot some before the sun sets tonight."

"Meanwhile, I have been working on scarecrow recipes," said Annalise.

Everyone turned to look at her and she gave a nervous smile.

"Is that food *for* scarecrows or food *made from* scarecrows?" Izzy asked. She wasn't sure which of those was the better option.

"Oh, nothing like that," said Annalise, alarmed. "It's more like a theme, so people can make party food to join in with the fun. Things like cheese straws served in a scarecrow hat, and decorated cupcakes with a scarecrow face."

Glenmore made a small harrumph of acknowledgement. "Well, our readership does seem to enjoy that sort of thing. Carry on. I assume Madame Zelda will have fresh horoscopes for the souvenir special?" he asked Izzy.

"She will get onto it immediately," said Izzy with a breezy grin. "She does love a souvenir edition, does Madame Zelda."

Glenmore fixed Izzy with a steely glare. They all pretended not to know that Izzy made up the horoscopes to suit her current thoughts on what specific people ought to be doing, but Glenmore's look was a warning not to take it too far. Izzy looked away, focusing on the plate of biscuits. She selected a bourbon.

"The final judging of the scarecrows, when they are displayed up at the castle for the big, ticketed event, will be the main focus. But of course we want behind-the-scenes interviews with the people of the town as they construct their masterpieces. We want to know the stories behind their choices. Everybody here can work on that."

There were nods all around.

"Lem and I are working on a joint creation. One of you can come and interview us," Glenmore continued.

Izzy put a hand in the air. "I will do that. It would be rude not to, really."

Nanna Lem was Izzy's grandma, as well as being Glenmore's dance partner (and possibly his girlfriend too, something else Izzy was not brave enough to investigate too deeply).

"Very good. Bring Garibaldi biscuits if you do," Glenmore said. "We've run out of those. We'll give you enough material for a front page story."

"Inside pages maybe," said Annalise gently. "It might be nice if we keep the front page for some actual news."

Glenmore grumbled a little. "Unless Izzy's dog manages to find another lost bag of cash in the street again, I doubt we're going to get another major front page story."

Izzy didn't point out that Monty wasn't exactly her dog and it had been Penny who'd been with Monty when he picked up the bag. It had been a tatty old cloth thing, stamped with the jester logo of an out of business casino in Great Yarmouth. In such an unremarkable bag had been several hundred pounds in loose bank notes. Where it had come from, Penny couldn't say, and perhaps most interesting of all, no one had come forward to claim it. The odd elements of the story (and Monty's photogenic nature) were enough for the Frambeat Gazette to make quite a big deal out of the story. It had even been picked up by a number of regional newspapers and news websites.

"You never know," said Annalise. "Maybe a big story will crop up in the next few days."

"Hardly likely," said Glenmore, fanning himself with several sheets of paper. "This isn't London. You're not going to get your big crime stories or scandals round here."

5

Penny picked her way around the edges of the mere, gently batting away any insects that drifted too close. They were hardly a nuisance. Everything moved with a lazy sluggishness in the orange light of evening.

On the far side there was a path leading up the side of the castle's dry moat to the bridge at the main entrance. Monty, off the lead, knew the way ahead perfectly and scampered up the little path. Penny looked back but could no longer see the camouflaged Belgian birdwatcher among the reeds and bushes.

There were many, many castles in England, large and small. A few were completely intact. Many were simply stone ruins on the ground. Framlingham castle had the benefits of being both large in scale and having walls that were very much still standing. It was true most of the inner buildings had been lost or replaced, and that many of the stairs and battlements had to be supported and made safe with modern materials, but Framlingham castle was a place where one could walk the high battlements and imagine what it would have been like to stand in this great Plantagenet fortress eight hundred years ago and survey the lands owned by the crown.

Unusually for a weekday evening, the gate to the castle was open and Monty scampered, unhindered, along the stone bridge and into the castle keep. Penny followed unhurriedly.

There were raised male voices within. In the centre of the large green space within the circling walls there was a great deal of equipment. A yet-to-be-erected marquee lay flat on the ground, and spaces all around the walls had been cordoned off. This would be where the scarecrows would be positioned during the opening day of the festival, and by the sound of it, it was scarecrows and their positioning causing the raised voices.

"…I am saying that as chair of the trustees of the castle, I have final say over placement of the competition entries—"

"And, as chair of the festival committee, you know I have been given carte blanche to lay things out as I see fit—"

"Within the bounds of health and safety as laid out by the trustees. To wit, me."

"To wit?"

"To wit."

"Are you a barn owl or something, Frank? You sound ridiculous."

The two arguers were Stuart Dinktrout and Frank Mountjoy. Frank, husband to dress shop owner Carmella, was a man who, in many ways, bore a certain resemblance to

Stuart. They were both successful businessmen of a certain age, both walked round in the obligatory wax jackets and Hunter boots of wealthy landowners, and both were loudly, even boorishly passionate about breeding little pigs for competitions. Yes, there were differences: Frank affected a somewhat posher accent and had a silver pencil moustache on his top lip, while Stuart had a strong propensity for showy ties and had the chocolatey voice of a cultured ladies' man (despite being resolutely single), but Penny had always thought the men were so alike they should be the best of friends. And yet they were squabbling rivals who, if the local stories were to be believed, frequently tried to have each other's pig disqualified in competition shows.

"And is having your wife's scarecrow placed here directly in front of the entrance a health and safety issue?" Stuart demanded.

"It is the ideal scarecrow for visitors to see as they enter," retorted Frank.

"Visitors and judges..."

Ah, thought Penny. It was as simple as that, the cause of their petty evening squabble.

"Well, it's not going there," said Stuart. "That's the tethering point for the inflatable pig."

"Inflatable pig?"

"Scarecrows are wired to their stations all around there, while here will be a floating balloon, welcoming visitors to the festival."

Indeed, currently deflated and laid out on the floor, was a huge pink pig. The words DINKTROUT GARDEN CENTRE were visible on its wrinkled plastic side.

"It's hideous," said Frank. "Modelled on your porcine princess no doubt."

"Arabella is far more beautiful than any hog you've raised. Suffolk Blimps did a wonderful job."

As the men squabbled, Penny saw movement on the battlements above, in the direction of the mere. Aubrey Jones spotted her and paused in the process of hanging strings of flags along the walls to wave at her. There was another tall, stout figure further along, but the dipping sun was behind them and Penny did not recognise the silhouette. She waved back vigorously to Aubrey.

There was a sudden buzzing to the side of her head. Penny was about to automatically swat the unseen insect aside when it turned out to be a dark, remote-controlled drone, swooping in from the castle gate. She saw Tariq Jazeel walking through with the controller in his hand.

"Sorry," he grinned foolishly. "Just getting used to the controls."

The sound had also drawn the attention of Stuart and Frank. They immediately dropped their argument in favour of someone else to berate.

"What's all this about?" demanded Frank.

"You don't have permission to be in here," said Stuart.

"I'm here to take pictures for the newspaper," said Tariq.

"Unannounced?" said Stuart.

Frank waved a hand to include Penny. "And this is no place to walk your doggy, madam! As I told that woman from Norfolk, we put out the open sign when we're open for visitors."

Frank gave no indication he had recognised Penny,

despite them having met before. But maybe a man who blithely called women half his age 'madam' didn't pay much attention to faces.

"I'm just collecting my 'doggy'," said Penny and went to shepherd Monty out of the gate.

"My old friend had a dog just like that," Frank called after her.

"Funny that," said Penny, but still the man failed to recognise her.

With a final wave up at Aubrey, who had returned to his flag-fixing duties, Penny went out of the castle.

"One lap of the castle and then home," she said. There was a foot route which wove above and within the moat. It was a good chance for a little dog to scamper in the grass without annoying self-important men.

As Penny reached the halfway point, she looked up at the ragged stone battlements thirty feet above her to see if she could spot Aubrey. There was no sign of him, but as she put her hand to her brow to shield it from the sun to look properly, there came a loud scream. It was a woman's scream, brief but joltingly piercing.

6

Monty's ears perked up in alarm.

"Round here!" said Penny and ran onwards around the wall.

On the mere-side of the castle there was no real moat and the land rose up to meet the castle wall. Partway down the slope was a figure, a body, dressed in a loose blue top and jeans. A blonde woman lying on her front with one arm bent awkwardly under herself and one leg crooked. There was a bit of furrowing in the earth, and a line of flattened grass where she must have hit the ground and rolled.

Penny looked up at the castle wall. Aubrey was staring down at her. Suddenly there was shouting from within the castle. Penny remembered herself and swiftly knelt at the woman's side.

"Hello? Hello? Are you all right?"

It was a blisteringly stupid question, but Penny didn't know what else to say to someone who had fallen off a castle wall. The woman wasn't moving. Her eyes were closed. Penny pushed her fingers against the woman's jawline and felt for a pulse. The woman's skin was warm but, as Penny felt around, she could find no signs of life.

"Okay, okay," she whispered to herself and took out her phone to call 999.

"Hello, what service do you require?"

"A woman has fallen off Framlingham castle wall. I think she's dead. Ambulance, I guess." She looked up again at the great height the woman had fallen from. "And police?"

BY THE TIME the air ambulance arrived, there was a small crowd around the woman's body.

The other figure up on the battlements with Aubrey had turned out to be Monica Blowers. The kind of woman who often uncharitably called 'big-boned'. She was a large woman, but physically active and very hands-on. She loved her off-road Land Rovers with a fanatical zeal and was more often seen with engine oil on her hands than not.

Seeing the woman on the ground, Monica had run down and methodically begun to go through the process of resuscitation: checking the woman's airways and starting the ultimately futile process of giving her chest compressions.

"You know CPR?" Penny had asked.

"Taught it to the scouts for years," said Monica. "I'd hope so."

By this time, the other people in the castle were also there. Aubrey and Tariq watched helplessly. When the helicopter began to descend onto nearby Castle Meadows, Stuart and Frank hurried over in a competitive effort to tell it where to land. Penny knew there was a certain type of man who couldn't let anyone park their car without getting involved and offering advice. She had no idea that also extended to emergency helicopters.

"You think she just fell?" Penny found herself asking no one at all.

Tariq looked up at the castle and shook his head. "The wall up there. It's well above waist height. You'd either have to be pushed or climb over it."

"Pushed?" The thought had never even occurred to Penny. "I wonder who she is?"

"Eve Bennefer," said Aubrey.

It took Penny a moment to recall the name. "The woman who just bought Pageant House?"

He nodded stiffly. "Only met her the once, but yeah, that's her."

The orange-suited ambulance paramedics came jogging up the path and took over from Monica. They asked quick and to-the-point questions they all tried to answer. Who she was. How she fell.

"Was anyone with her?" asked one paramedic.

Penny, Aubrey, Tariq, Monica, Stuart and Frank all looked at one another.

"No," said Aubrey eventually. "She must have been alone."

"I told her we weren't open," said Frank. "I thought she'd left."

The ambulance crew had brought a body board stretcher

with them, but within a few minutes they'd confirmed there was no sign of life at all and radioed it in.

Somehow, everyone found themselves back up on the main driveway. Distant sirens told them the police were on their way.

Penny leaned against the wall, holding Monty to her chest, and looked past the helicopter parked on the field to the extensive back gardens of Pageant House.

"Just bought it?" she said.

Aubrey took a moment to catch up. He nodded. "Bought for cash, I hear. The woman had money."

She sighed. "Maybe money doesn't bring happiness."

Aubrey placed a comforting arm around her shoulder. "You never really know people, do you?"

Blue police lights appeared along Church Street. There would be a lot of questions to answer before anyone went home.

7

Izzy had popped in to see Nanna Lem in her little flat after the Frambeat Gazette meeting and then she rode her bicycle home. It was an old-fashioned women's bike, and she had added to its existing charms with a liberal amount of yarn-bombing. The frame, the sit-up-and-beg handlebars, even some of the spokes, were decorated with bright stripy sections of wool. For a woman who preferred any creative activities over the accumulation of actual possessions, the bike was probably her favourite object in the whole world.

However, cycling around in the heat of summer was perhaps less than delightful. It was so hot there was a balance needing to be struck between the welcome breeze generated by moving more swiftly and the overheating caused by pedalling. Izzy compromised by riding at the most leisurely pace she could manage without falling off.

Izzy lived at the farmhouse and dog training centre

operated by her boyfriend. Izzy King and Marcin Nowak had only been an item for a matter of months, so their domestic routine was a relatively new thing, and they still hit occasional bumps.

Izzy approached the kitchen door, which was the back door of the farmhouse, and the one they routinely used. The door split into two, like a stable door, which Izzy had only found out when the weather grew warmer. It still made her smile, especially when one of Marcin's taller dogs peered over the bottom half, like now, tongue lolling in greeting.

"Hello Skidoo!" she said as she approached. "You think you're a horse?"

Marcin appeared and opened the bottom part of the door for her. "Good evening! I have made us some chilled soup, as it's so warm."

"Yum!" Izzy loved Marcin's cooking, especially when he made dishes from his native Poland. "Is it the kind of soup that comes with dumplings?"

Marcin rolled his eyes. "I am aware of your fondness for *uszka*, so yes it is!"

As they sat and enjoyed their meal, they chatted about their day. Izzy explained the scarecrow making that had boosted the footfall into the shop.

"So, you and Penny are also making a scarecrow?" asked Marcin.

"We hadn't necessarily planned to..." she began.

"But?" he said, knowing there was a 'but'.

"Carmella Mountjoy came into the shop."

"Oh, that Carmella. Did she, um, rile you up?"

"She might have accused us of making voodoo dolls."

"Again?"

"Again. And she was bragging about entering the scarecrow competition herself."

"She herself will be a scarecrow?" Marcin frowned as he halved one of his ear-shaped dumplings.

"Not entering *herself* herself," said Izzy. "Although that is a fun image. No, she is going to construct an entry."

"And so now you must also do the same."

"Er, yes. We will. Although we haven't started yet, with all of the other stuff going on. I thought we might chat about it today, but Penny was busy sorting out the permit for our table on the pavement."

"Regulations cannot be ignored," said Marcin. "I have been looking into what's needed for us to have sheep and there are things to be done there."

Izzy grinned in adoration. "Sheep!"

The arrival of sheep at their little smallholding was the culmination of a sequence of events which had started with something as small as Izzy finding cheap fleeces on the internet. Marcin had then surprised her by buying some wool processing equipment from an old mill in Wales. It had initially been a glorious misunderstanding, where Marcin had enquired about a loom and had ended up with an enormous carding machine as well. He had coaxed it into life in the barn with the help of some friends. The purchase of a carding machine then led to some extra equipment for gilling, combing, roving and spinning (and some books so Izzy and Marcin could learn words like 'gilling' and 'roving'). Then they realised several thousand pounds of equipment in the old barn would not be kept busy for long with just a few cheap fleeces. And so ... sheep!

"Just imagine how fantastic that will be," said Izzy. "Whatever admin is needed, I can help."

"Knowing how much you hate admin makes me realise that you are very committed to this idea," smiled Marcin. "This makes me very happy."

Izzy thrilled at the idea of sheep being a part of their life; she could see how they might make it into an exciting new business venture. "Taking wool from sheep to sweater could be just the most amazing thing ever. I am very excited to make it happen," she said as her phone began to ring.

"And so we will Izzy," declared Marcin.

Izzy looked at her phone. It was Penny calling. She answered. "Hello?"

"Are you busy?" Penny's voice was quiet, withdrawn.

"I've got about one and a half dumplings to go."

"I've just witnessed something awful."

"What is it?"

"I found a body."

"You found a body?"

"Is it Carmella's?" asked Marcin as he ate.

Izzy silently shushed him. "You need me to come over?"

"No," said Penny quickly. *"But I need someone to talk to."*

"Anytime," said Izzy. She pushed her chair away from the table and went into the living room to settle down for a good long listen.

8

Izzy arrived at the shop the following morning with foamy chocolate sprinkled coffee (with extra sprinkles). She was a firm believer that sweet delights were as good a remedy for shock as anything else, and by what Penny had managed to convey last night, she had indeed had something of a shock.

She put the coffees on the counter, gave Monty a bit of a fuss and then gave her cousin a big hug.

"What's that for?" Penny laughed.

"Sometimes you just deserve a hug."

"There are times I don't?"

"Oh, I'm sure there are. Sleep okay?"

Penny took the lid off her coffee and blew away the steam. "I did. Woke early. I did that thing where I just kept playing over in my mind whether I could have done something different."

"Stopped the woman leaping off the castle wall?"

"I could have been quicker, done something."

"You saw her fall."

"Heard her. Heard her and ran. I was the first one there but I'm not sure I—" She tutted irritably at herself. "Of course, I did all I could. It's just so very sad."

"It is."

"The police have sealed off that bit of the ramparts while they work out what happened. Monica and Aubrey were up there and they saw no one with the woman. Not even sure they realised she was up there too."

"Suicide then?"

"I guess but…" She laughed, a little sadly. "Such a cliché. She seemed to have everything to live for. Bought that Pageant House place next to Castle Meadows. Paid cash for it, Aubrey said. So she had money, a nice house. I think she was an attractive woman." She laughed at herself again. "I'm not saying money, possessions and good looks equal happiness!"

Izzy nodded gently. "I know what you mean. People's lives can seem so positive."

Penny drank her coffee and murmured softly in pleasure.

"Of course, Pageant House is cursed," said Izzy.

"What? No, it's not."

"Yes, it is. Hardly anyone's ever lived in it for more than a couple of years. The last couple were driven out by the ghost in the attic."

"What?" said Penny, incredulous.

"The ghost in the attic."

"You don't believe in ghosts!"

"Who says I don't believe in ghosts?"

"I thought you were a completely sane and rational human—" Penny stopped herself. "Obviously, I don't think you're a completely sane and rational human being, Izzy King. I've known you too long. But ghosts? Who believes in ghosts in this day and age?"

"Madame Zelda believes in ghosts," said Izzy.

"*You* are Madame Zelda!"

"Madame Zelda is a carefully crafted persona who happens to believe in ghosts."

"And you do too?"

"I don't *not* believe in ghosts," said Izzy. "There's too many stories to dismiss them all. Fram is full of ghosts. Like Black Boots."

Penny's lips were frozen in a querying 'o'. "Who, pray tell, is Black Boots?"

"You've not heard of Black Boots?"

"Clearly not."

"It's a ghost up at the castle. Some say he's a medieval knight or a soldier from the civil war, but all anyone who's ever seen him can agree on—"

"—is he's wearing black boots."

"You've seen him too?" said Izzy, her eyes sparkling with mischief.

Penny grinned and shook her head. "The things you come out with sometimes."

Izzy gave a little bow. "I am here to entertain." She produced a sheet of paper with a flourish. "Speaking of entertainment, I know how much you love a list, so I made one of possible scarecrows we could make."

"Oh, we're definitely making one?"

"Can't have Carmella Mountjoy beating us to the prize. This list can kickstart our brainstorming session."

"Yes, you're right," said Penny. "And we really should make a start today or we'll run out of time."

Izzy watched Penny's face as she scanned the list of possibilities.

"Um, what would a scarecrow horse look like, exactly?" Penny asked, looking up.

"Hah! It would be like a pantomime horse, so you would have it made from two scarecrows, one of them bending over." It seemed like such an obvious idea, but Izzy could tell Penny was having trouble visualising it. "Well, never mind the four-legged ones then—"

"—There are quite a lot of them," said Penny. "Especially when scarecrows don't really have legs anyway."

"Fine. Let's move on. What do you think about some of the other ideas?"

"I think I like the section about famous women best," said Penny.

"Not the animals one?" said Izzy, slightly disappointed. "A meercat would be fun."

"No, let's stick with people. I know it's nice to, um, push the envelope, but I think everyone will be expecting people. So how would you do some of these? Madame Curie for example – how would I know it was her specifically?"

"She would be holding a glowing test tube," said Izzy.

"Hm. Yes. There might be health and safety issues there. We need to make it clear who the person is without adding elements that children might cut themselves on."

"Mary Hunt then? She's next in the list."

"Who's she?"

"She was Alexander Fleming's lab assistant. All we need for her is a mouldy melon. It would be educational! We grow a spectacular bloom of mould on the melon and show everyone how penicillin was invented. She was the one who sourced it for Fleming's lab."

"No," said Penny firmly. "I think it needs to be a general 'no' to anything that involves mouldy melons. And maybe we need someone who is more well-known?"

Izzy grunted with frustration. "But she *should* be well known! Society has celebrated Fleming and forgotten Mary."

Penny had gone back to the list. "Here's a better possibility, the artist Frida Kahlo! She would be fun to do. Is she famous enough?"

"Sure. Maybe not everyone knows her name but if you say 'that Mexican artist woman with the eyebrows' everyone would know who you mean," said Izzy. "She had a very distinctive look, and we could dress her up in one of her famous *huipils*."

"Her famous what?"

"The *huipil* is a Mexican garment, like a tunic. If you picture Frida Kahlo, she would usually be wearing one over a long skirt."

"Yes, that does sound nice. They are very colourful clothes, too, aren't they?"

"They are!" Izzy jigged with excitement.

Penny narrowed her eyes. "Did you put all this other stuff on here just to make me seize upon the only thing that makes sense, which is the one you really wanted to do anyway?"

"Not at all!" Izzy put a hand to her heart in mock horror. "Anyway, this was just a jumping-off point. Maybe you've got other ideas."

Penny picked up Monty's lead from the side. "We will do a quick walk while the weather's still bearable and maybe I will think of something. Assuming I don't get surprised by any strange men on the mere today."

"Pardon?"

Penny described how she came to meet Remi the birdwatcher. "He seemed quite an interesting guy," she finished.

"Don't get many Belgians come through here," said Izzy. "Although why you stopped to talk to him when he was a bit rude to you and Monty seems odd."

Penny's cheeks turned pink. "I just thought he was interesting!

Izzy looked at her more intently. "You need to explain yourself. Is that 'Oh look, he has a unusual fabric-based apparatus, I wonder what it is?' interesting, or is it more like 'Oh look, a hot stranger is in town, I must engage him in conversation and arrange to meet him again' interesting?"

"You are terrible, Izzy! And you must stop calling every single man under thirty 'hot'."

"So, he's single then?" said Izzy playfully.

"I don't know!"

"He was handsome then?"

"Not exactly," said Penny but the crimson depth to her cheeks told its own story. "I'm not sure I can explain what was attractive about him. Something in his eyes. A dreamer."

"He's dreamy, is he?"

"I said he looked like a dreamer, Izzy!"

Izzy smiled. "Well, let's hope he does call in then. If he's staying in the College Road holiday lodges he might call early, before the birds are up."

Penny laughed. "I'm pretty sure birds get up super early."

9

Izzy was setting up the scarecrow-making table outside the shop when she saw a man walking up Market Hill carrying something that looked like a small tent under one arm.

She took a moment to look at him while he checked the name of the shop to be sure he had found the right place. He wore a bucket hat with a small feather tucked into the band, the brim worn low over his brow so Izzy couldn't check his eyes until he got a little closer. They were blue-grey, edged with dark lashes. They looked like the eyes of a dreamer.

"This is Cozy Craft, yes?" he asked Izzy.

"Penny's just out with her dog. She'll be back soon."

He frowned at her. "Ah, Penny. So, this *is* the place?"

"Very much the right place," said Izzy and steered him inside.

Penny returned five minutes later and her face split in a slightly panicked grin when she saw the newcomer.

"I've just been showing Remi here some of our scarecrow ideas," said Izzy.

"I like Frida Kahlo," he said. "She also liked birds."

"Had a pet parrot called Bonito, apparently," Izzy added helpfully.

Penny, foolish grin still on her face, nodded like she didn't know what do with that information. Remi stood in the middle of the floor between the two women and didn't seem to know what to do either. Izzy could feel the awkwardness pouring off them. She had no idea if that represented some form of romantic tension but she loved it.

"What's this you've brought?" she asked pointedly, gesturing at the tent drooping from his grasp.

"This? This is called the Wanderhide and I don't like it," said Remi. "I wanted something that would be easy to carry and discreet to erect, but this does not work well."

"I mentioned that Remi was struggling with his hide," said Penny, finally leaping into the conversation.

"Could we maybe take it outside and you can show us how it works?" said Izzy.

"Yes, I can."

On the pavement, Remi put the small tent thing down and expanded the flexible poles until it stood tall, like a sentry box.

"Ooh I see." Izzy unzipped it and stood inside. "What am I doing in here if I am birdwatching? Is this a little window to see out of?"

"Yes, but it's all wrong. It's made of plastic that has gone all cloudy, so I can't see out, even with my eyes."

"Even with your eyes?" Izzy wondered what the alternative might be.

"I mean, with the naked eye, is that the correct phrase? There is no possibility to use binoculars or a camera. Also, it assumes I am standing up, while I would prefer to sit when I can. It can be a time consuming wait so this is not appropriate." He tugged at the camera hanging round his neck. "My photographs from yesterday. They are only so-so."

"Oh I see," said Izzy, ducking up and down, trying to picture herself waiting for a bird to come along. "It would be better if there was a little opening, positioned ... around about here."

"Yes it would."

Izzy emerged from the tent and walked around the outside. "We could add that in for you: a little slot, with a flap that covers it up maybe?"

"That would be an improvement, it's true," said Remi with a small nod. "It would make it much more useable once I am in place. Getting into place is very disruptive. The people who made this have never been out in the field with it, I am certain."

"Tell us about the difficulties that you have," said Penny. "It sounds—"

Penny never got to finish her thought, because Stuart Dinktrout chose that moment to announce his presence with a growl of outrage. "What on earth is going on here?"

"I am showing them my inappropriate hide, sir," said Remi.

That sentence flummoxed Stuart for several moments. "I think I have gone out on a limb for you already," he said to Penny and Izzy. "I've agreed to fast track your application for a table out here, and now I see that you're setting up some sort of horrible festival tent! It is an outrage!"

"Stuart, I am sorry but it's not that at all," said Penny. "Remi here is a customer, or he might be anyway. He was simply showing us the shortcomings of his bird hide."

"Bird hide, eh?" Stuart said, walking around it. "Never saw anything like this before."

Remi shrugged. "It is not very good."

"Well, make sure you take it down immediately," said Stuart. "I'm keeping my eye on you two."

All three of them watched Stuart Dinktrout walk away.

"That man, he is your father?"

"No," said Izzy.

"A grumpy uncle?"

"Not even close," said Penny.

"Ah, he is the *bemoeial*, the, er, person who goes around just telling people what to do for no good reason."

"Busybody," Penny laughed.

"Yes. Busybody." Remi sighed and grasped the edges of his tent. "What a strange man. I will take it down, but here, let me show you one of the problems. Sometimes I want to move a short distance away, yes? What I might do is pick it up like this and carry it, but see how it catches the wind, even a slight breeze? It will snag on trees and other things too. It is so tall, it's ridiculous."

"Especially if you're normally sitting down in it," said Izzy. "It would be better if you chopped it in half and carried the top half on your shoulders."

They all laughed at the idea, as Remi folded the tent into a manageable bundle.

"Cup of tea?" Penny asked Remi, a lightness to her tone that didn't fool Izzy for one minute. Having overcome the flustered surprise of having an attractive newcomer on her doorstep, she was going on the offensive.

"Yes please. I never refuse when a British person offers tea. It is a rule, yes?"

"Surprisingly close to the truth," said Penny.

10

They went back inside the shop and Penny made drinks for them all.

"Do you use your little tent to make cups of tea?" asked Penny, as she passed Remi a cup.

"No, I would take a drink in a flask. Its purpose is to disguise me from the birds as I use my camera and binoculars. And to keep me dry as well."

"Huh," said Izzy. "So a little shoulder tent is almost what you need. Almost."

"Yes, I am afraid my shoulders are not so large that they could support a tent," said Remi with a smile. He drained his tea and gathered up his tent. "It was very good of you to think about my problems, but perhaps this is simply unsolvable."

"We're not out of ideas yet, are we?" said Penny. As Remi bent towards his tent bundle, she mouthed *Think of something!* at Izzy.

"Of course we're not out of ideas," said Izzy loudly. Her

mind raced. She worked well under pressure, but she had nothing. She pictured Remi with a stubby tent on his shoulders, which was an amusing but unrealistic image.

Penny pulled an exaggerated sad face, as she could see Izzy was drawing a blank.

"Wait!" A picture popped into Izzy's head and she blinked at the abrupt certainty that she had a solution. "I need to show you a picture." She went to the counter and rifled through the reference materials sitting on the shelves underneath. It was a collection of books and cuttings, both old and modern, that contained everything from details of particular sewing techniques to fashion collections and exhibitions. The particular thing she had in mind was in a book that had been issued by a museum. No more than a pamphlet really.

"Couldn't we just look on the internet for a picture?" asked Penny, after Izzy had been searching in vain for a few minutes.

"We could, if I could remember the correct word to search for. It's here somewhere!" Izzy pulled out a thick wodge of papers that had been pulled out of magazines. There, stuck between an article on macramed plant pot holders and a sheet of eighteenth century knitting styles, was the pamphlet she needed. "Here it is!"

She walked round to the others as she flicked through the pages and laid the booklet out on the counter.

"See this picture?" She pointed at the page.

"It's just a bonnet," said Penny. "I mean it's lovely, like the sort of thing they might have worn in *Pride and Prejudice*, but I don't see how it's helping us."

"Yep, yep – but it's the construction we're interested in. It is called a calash, and it was designed to protect the fancy hairdos of aristocrats with giant hair. This one here is a reasonable sort of size, but look at this cartoon over the page. It's mocking how massive these hairdos got, and the calashes."

"This is most interesting," said Remi, as Izzy turned the page and showed the line drawing reproduced there. It was of a woman wearing a tall coiffure, and a bonnet that extended right over it, high above her head.

"The calash is designed to pull up when you need the protection, then fold backwards, out of the way, when you don't," said Izzy. "It's a bit like the hood of an old-fashioned pram."

"So you could make a bird hide version," said Penny. "This is a fantastic idea, Izzy. How were they constructed?"

"I will look into that, but I am certain we can do something," said Izzy.

"What do you think, Remi?" asked Penny.

Remi smiled. "Truthfully? I came in here to be polite, because you invited me. I did not expect to be involved in the development of a brand new design of bird hide. I want to see one of these things. Can you really make one?"

"Yes," said Penny. She turned and looked at Izzy. "We can do this, can't we? Get Remi a better hide so he can take better photos."

Izzy nodded. "We can. We'll get a design, a quote, and get right onto it."

"And maybe you'll have more joy spotting the white-tipped lapwing," said Penny.

"White-*tailed* lapwing," he corrected. "So far, I have only taken some very mediocre pictures of some very common birds."

He slipped the camera off his neck and angled it so she could see the preview screen built into the rear. "Some great crested grebes."

"These are beautiful! So professional. Look, Izzy."

Izzy peered at the screen and couldn't help but agree. She was struck by how crisp and precise the images were. Remi's camera had caught every ripple of the water, had brought the reed beds so perfectly into focus.

Remi shrugged. "Very ordinary pictures I'm afraid. Enough to use as reference for my sketches. The grebes have better plumage in the spring."

Penny attracted their attention with a flapping of her hand. "How do you zoom in on this?" She had been flicking through the pictures on the camera screen and something had clearly caught her eye.

"The little buttons in the top right," Remi said, reaching with his hand over hers to show her. "This picture? The bird is almost entirely out of shot."

"No. Behind it."

Izzy peered in from the other side. It was, amongst a number of impressive shots, a haphazard snap of a white waterbird in flight.

"Zoom in," said Penny, pressing the button for herself.

The image captured the land and sky looking across the mere to the castle, and Izzy could see that Penny wanted to zoom in on the castle behind. Even with high resolution the walls became increasingly blurry as she expanded the image.

"When was this taken?" asked Penny.

"There is the time stamp," said Remi. "Six fourteen p.m."

"It's accurate?"

"For sure," he said.

Penny took her phone out and scrolled. Izzy could see she was looking at her phone dialling record. Penny put her phone on the counter. She'd dialled 999 at six twenty-one p.m.: seven minutes after the photo was taken.

"Am I meant to be seeing something?" said Izzy.

With nervous fingers, Penny zoomed in once more and pointed at the small screen. There was the dirty yellow stone of the castle wall, the blue sky above, and now Izzy could see what Penny was pointing at. There were two blurry figures on the battlements. Rough blurry figures, but definitely two humans.

"That was where she fell from," Penny said softly.

"Who?" said Remi.

"The woman, Eve. Aubrey and Monica were up there. Different places, but they said there was no one else up there. They were sure the woman had to be alone." Penny looked at Izzy, with a fierce searching gaze. "But there *was* someone on the wall with Eve Bennefer."

Izzy didn't know what to say.

"Black Boots?" she suggested.

11

Just before breaking for lunch, Penny looked over Izzy's shoulder at the sketch of what a birdwatching calash might look like. Monty snoozed at their feet in his little basket, although every time "bird" was mentioned his feet pedalled as if he was dreaming about chasing them.

"I've done some research," said Izzy. "The hoops were made from bent cane or whalebone. I wonder if there's a gardening thing that uses bent canes?"

Penny thought about that. "Your mum would be the best person to ask. I was thinking though, you know those super-flexible tent poles you can get? What about those?"

Izzy turned and gave her a penetrating look. "You're right. They would be perfect. In fact, starting this whole thing with the pieces of a tent would be a good idea, there are bound to be things we could re-use."

"Tents are mostly in brighter colours though. We should probably budget for some camouflage nylon."

They scribbled notes, checked prices, and Izzy completed the sketches that would form the basis for the design.

"Did Glenmore once help organise the local Scout group?" Izzy said.

Penny had no idea. She'd lived most of her life outside Fram and only returned recently. "He might be able to hook us up with an old tent," she conceded.

"Glenmore said that he and Nanna Lem were making a joint scarecrow," said Izzy. "I think I am supposed to interview them for the Frambeat Gazette."

"We can multi-task," said Penny.

∽

PENNY AND IZZY strolled to Miller Fields sheltered accommodation together.

"Remi seems nice," Izzy said casually. "I can see why you're crushing on him."

"Am I twelve? Crushing on him? Seriously Izzy!"

"You're not crushing on him?"

Penny gave her a stern look, although Izzy was wearing a floppy sun hat and it was nearly impossible to make eye contact. "I don't need a man in my life to make me complete."

"Never said you did."

"But some adult company would be nice." Penny realised what she'd said and felt the need to qualify it. "I mean, when I say adult, I just mean mature."

"Oh, I'm sure he's matured," said Izzy innocently.

"I mean a normal human being who doesn't accuse me of 'crushing' on someone, or who doesn't think that a ghost called Black Boots pushed a woman off the castle wall."

"I didn't say Black Boots pushed her. I just said Black Boots is real."

At Miller's Field, they found Nanna Lem and Glenmore in the lounge. It was normally a tidy place, where the residents would sit quietly and chat or read books. Sometimes there were crafting sessions and other activity, but Izzy didn't think she had ever seen it in quite such a state of chaos.

"Holy moly, this is amazing! It's like everyone at Miller Fields has got scarecrow fever!" breathed Izzy.

"Hello girls, come to see where it's all happening?" called Nanna Lem, eighty years young, standing at the head of a huge row of trestle tables. The various stages of scarecrow construction were arranged in stations at the tables, like a production line.

"Wow Nanna," said Penny, pausing to give her grandma a peck on the cheek. "It's good to see everyone involved."

"We made a sign-up sheet and got so many names that we were able to arrange bulk purchases on some of the materials," said Glenmore, stalking down the line of tables as if he was a major overseeing a military operation. "We have turned over the use of the lounge to scarecrow production for the week. Nobody really objected."

A woman in the far corner looked up from her book as if she was thinking about voicing an objection, but she lowered her eyes again and gave a small sigh.

"We came for two reasons," said Izzy. "I need to interview you for the Frambeat Gazette, but I'll just use some snippets from our conversation, we don't need to make it too formal. The other thing is a commission we're looking at doing. We might want to see if anyone has an old tent we can experiment with. One of the ones with flexible poles."

"Planning on spending a night under canvas?" said Glenmore. "Excellent."

"Actually, this is more of a sewing experiment."

His expression immediately soured.

"But the aim is to help create practical and portable camouflage," Penny pointed out.

This piqued his interest again. "Does it need any particular features other than flexible poles?" asked Glenmore.

"No. We plan to replace the fabric," said Penny.

"I may have just the thing for you then. Miss Blowers has taken over with the scouts group in recent years. You know her? Volunteers at the Community Change shop. She had one of those pop-up tents recently. All gone at the seams. Worth asking her if she's still got it."

"Superb," said Izzy.

Penny waved her hand over the construction around them. "Tell us about your scarecrow, then. We might be making one of our own soon."

"Actually, ours is scarecrows, plural," said Nanna Lem. "They are not finished, but I think we can show them to you."

Lem and Glenmore shuffled behind a nearby trestle table and went into a conspiratorial huddle. When they emerged, they were each carrying a scarecrow. Glenmore's only had one arm, so he wedged one end of the scarecrow's outstretched arm into his left shoulder and held the other end with his right hand. His scarecrow wore top hat and tails, while Nanna Lem's wore a long gown and had a blonde wig.

"Now, we need to position ourselves correctly," said Nanna Lem.

They adjusted their stance, so that the two scarecrows were locked in an embrace, and it became clear that their legs were positioned to give the illusion they were dance partners.

"Oh wow, they are an old-time dancing couple!" said Izzy.

"Yes, but who?" asked Nanna Lem.

"Is it Ryan Gosling and Emma Stone in *La La Land*?" asked Penny.

"I don't know who that is," said Glenmore with a frown. "It's Fred Astaire and Ginger Rogers."

"I thought Fred Astaire was a tennis player," said Izzy.

Glenmore huffed. "Don't young people watch films anymore?"

"Well, to be fair, *La La Land* is a film," said Penny. "And it's one we are more likely to have seen. You should watch it, I think you might like it."

"Getting back to the interview questions," said Izzy. "What made you want to create this particular pair of scarecrows?"

Nanna Lem exchanged a fond glance with Glenmore. "We're romantic fools—"

"I'm romantic, she's the fool," said Glenmore.

"—and we love to dance. We all grew up knowing that Fred and Ginger were the greatest dance partnership, and everyone wanted to be them. It was the obvious choice for us."

Glenmore gave a stiff smile. He didn't look much like a romantic fool to Izzy's eyes, and yet here he was.

"Lovely," said Izzy. "And where did their outfits come from?"

"The gown is one of mine from years ago," said Nanna Lem. "Fred's tux is rented, and so is the top hat. Those will need to go back after the display."

"We're going to need a picture of you two dancing in the same pose, next to your scarecrow counterparts," said Izzy. "That will set off the interview nicely. We'll get Tariq to take the picture as he's the official photographer."

They spent a while admiring the scarecrow-building efforts around the lounge.

"You ever heard of Black Boots?" Penny asked idly.

"Of course," said Glenmore. "A guard or something, wasn't he? Roaming the stairs in search of his gold."

"I thought he was a prisoner who is seen walking up to the prison tower and then falling to the dungeon," said Nanna Lem.

"No, that's a different ghost, I'm sure."

"There's multiple ghosts?" said Penny.

"It's an old castle," said Glenmore. "A lot of history."

Penny hummed thoughtfully. "I thought you'd be a bit more rational than that, Glenmore."

"Oh, I believe there are things beyond our reckoning, girl," he said. "Did you know, the palm of my hand itches every time my lottery numbers are about to come up?"

"Pure chance," Penny suggested.

Glenmore held up his one hand. "Thing is, it's not this hand that itches."

Despite the muggy warmth of the day, Penny felt a momentary chill run through her.

12

They dropped in on the Community Change charity shop on their way back to Cozy Craft. The shop was several doors down the hill from their own business, occupying a narrow but deep building at the point where Market Hill became Bridge Street.

Penny saw that one of Monica Blowers' Land Rovers was parked in the marketplace parking spot nearest the shop. Her eyes were drawn to the deep parallel scratch marks along its rear corner.

"I hope that's not recent or she's not going to be in a good mood," noted Izzy, who had also seen the scratches.

The charity shop's window display was full of children's toys and an eclectic array of paintings and wall art. Inside was an even more eclectic and cluttered emporium of second-hand goods. There was some degree of order – women's clothes here, a book section there, a solid wall of unwanted DVDs over there – but each section looked ready to explode into the next. Monica was behind the counter and, more specifically, behind a wall of bin bags and boxes full of donated material.

"No more donations," the woman said automatically. "We just don't have room."

"We come bearing no gifts of any sort," said Izzy cheerily.

Monica finally looked at them and smiled in recognition. "We are snowed under here, which in one sense is wonderful and in another sense is..." She grimaced. "Every morning, I arrive and find people have dumped their donations in front of the door, like it's rubbish."

"I've noticed," said Penny.

"It's not how we work," Monica muttered, "but they still do it, no matter how many signs we put up." She forced herself to present a happier face. "But I shouldn't complain. Everything we sell is more money for the meals on wheels and the free hospital taxi service."

"I hear you're hoping to raise money for a new minibus," said Izzy.

"That's the dream. The proceeds from the scarecrow event just might get us over the line. I've got my eye on a reconditioned minibus in Woodbridge. I'd have that up and running in no time. Now, please tell me you've come here to buy something. I'm willing to sell stuff in bulk by the kilo."

"Well, we're certainly hoping to take something away," said Penny and did her best to explain their tent request.

"So, you want a tent but don't want to use it as a tent?"

"We're going to put it to creative use," said Izzy.

Monica had been the recipient of one of Cozy Craft's more extravagant designs when she went to a wedding the previous winter in a fancy, swan-themed costume. She knew full well what Penny and Izzy were capable of.

She disappeared into a back room and, after a modicum of huffing and thrashing, came back out with a flat tent, folded into a sort of circular configuration.

"One pop-up tent, totally jiggered at the seams," she said. "Five quid to you."

"A bargain," said Izzy, happy to put some money in the charity's till.

"Anything else you want to buy while you're here?" Monica suggested hopefully.

Penny browsed the racks while Izzy gazed at some of the trinkets in the glass-covered counter.

"You should sell mystery boxes," said Izzy.

"What's that then?" said Monica.

"You know, box up some things. A book, a hat, an ornament and a jigsaw, then seal it up for punters to buy unseen."

"Don't reckon many people will buy stuff they haven't seen," said Monica.

"Theme them. Men, women, young, old. Whatever. A pound a go, I bet they'd go like hot cakes at Christmas."

Monica laughed. "It's August!"

"Trust Izzy to come up with killer Christmas ideas in summer," said Penny as she pulled a jacket from the rack. "Hey. This is nice."

The jacket was made from a sturdy cotton fabric and embroidered top to bottom with bold patches of colour that morphed into big blooming flowers over the lapels and chest.

"That came in this morning," said Monica. "Only just put

it out."

"More daring than you'd usually wear," Izzy said.

"It's got a bit of a Latin American vibe," said Penny. "Wondering if I should buy it for myself or if we use it to dress Frida."

"Frida?" said Monica.

"Frida Kahlo. She's our scarecrow."

"Or will be," said Izzy.

"Ring it up. And this." Penny placed a DVD of *Top Hat* on the counter. "Fred Astaire and Ginger Rogers," she said to Izzy.

"Classic of the genre," said Monica. "Mistaken identity and misplaced outrage. Lots of fun."

Penny was surprised. "Never saw you as the musical-loving type."

"Think I've got a Land Rover piston instead of a human heart?" she said.

The answer "yes" wanted to spring to Penny's lips, but she held herself. "Speaking of beloved vehicles, you do know you've got a scratch on—"

She didn't even get to the end of the sentence before a great rumbling growl of annoyance burbled and boiled from within Monica.

"I was bloody livid when I saw that," she chuntered. "Bloody scratches. The eighty-three Land Rover Defender is a sturdy beast. She can take it. But to do that to a parked car and then drive off. No note, no nothing."

"Oh, that is annoying," said Izzy sympathetically, although not summoning the same level of offended outrage Monica was exhibiting.

"Downright anti-social. If I ever catch the person who did it..." Monica made a throttling gesture with her two powerful hands, thumbs pressed into the windpipe of her invisible victim.

"Let's hope you don't then, eh?" said Penny.

Monica tutted and let her hands drop. "Who'd run this place or keep the scout troop going if I went to prison for murder?"

"Exactly."

Penny carried the DVD and jacket. Izzy took the tent.

"Enjoy the film!" said Monica. "Look at how many ostrich feathers Ginger loses from her costume in the final routine. They clearly didn't have dressmakers like you back in them days."

Penny waggled the DVD in response. "Oh, and thank you, for yesterday," she said.

"Yesterday?"

"At the castle."

Monica frowned as though she had genuinely forgotten and then her eyebrows went up. "Oh, that. Did what I could, didn't I?"

"Did everything she could to save that woman's life," Penny said to Izzy.

"But, alas, it was not meant to be," Monica added coolly.

Penny thought of Remi's camera image, of the two shadowy figures on the battlement. "And you didn't see anyone with her beforehand?" she asked.

"Didn't even know she was up there," said Monica. "No one came by me."

13

As soon as they were back in Cozy Craft, Izzy was keen to check out the tent's potential. "We can't give your Remi a proper quote until we're sure we can make his wearable bird hide."

"I quite agree," said Penny. "And he's not my Remi. I'm just going to put these upstairs."

While Penny was gone, Izzy picked up the large circular bag and unzipped it around the edge. She slid out the folded tent, wondering if it would be big enough for what they needed. As it came free, she found that the looped poles in her hand slid apart. She separated them slightly, and the tent took over. Before she knew what was happening, it had burst into its three dimensional shape.

Monty, startled by the appearance of a giant orange thing in his home, started barking.

"Oh crumbs!" Izzy exclaimed. It had quite taken her by

surprise. She hadn't realised that 'pop-up tent' meant just that, and it would pop up all by itself.

"What's wrong?" shouted Penny from upstairs.

"Erm, nothing too bad," said Izzy.

Penny came thumping down the stairs. "When you say it's not too bad, I know it's probably bad. Oh, my—" Penny had to stop at the foot of the stairs as the tent filled much of the floorspace. "How big is that thing? And why have you put it up in here?"

"So many questions!" said Izzy. "First of all, I did not put it up in here."

"I think you did."

"It put itself up!"

"Right…"

"I did not expect it to do that. Second of all, I had no idea it was going to be this massive. It's like magic how a tent as big as this could fit into a flat circle."

The tent had erected itself in a space that wasn't really large enough for its footprint. It lolloped over some upright rolls of fabric, and its corner was wedged up inside the window display.

"Maybe I'll just fold it up again and I can look at it in a different place," said Izzy.

"Good idea. How do you fold it up?"

"I, erm, I have no idea," said Izzy. "Can you ask Monica?"

"I can't get to the door. There's a tent and an idiot cousin in the way."

"Well, it's got me trapped in this corner. Have you got her number?"

While Penny attempted to get hold of Monica, Izzy tried to seize the tent's poles, certain they were the key to this. She could hold them all in her hand, but still the tent billowed and flopped.

"You know what this is like? It's like trying to fold a fitted sheet, but one with attitude and poles." Izzy tried using her bodyweight to flatten the whole thing, but she ended up rolling on the floor while the thing popped up to either side.

She wrestled to her feet, marvelling at the tent's power to reform itself no matter what she did.

Penny had Monica on the phone. "Yes, yes, Izzy did put it up in the shop. No, she has no idea what to do next." Penny pulled the phone away from her ear. "It is quite funny I suppose. Sorry what—? Photos? I'm not sure Izzy wants me to take her photo."

Izzy stared at the ceiling, waiting.

"Er, Izzy?" Penny called. "Monica says she will only tell you what to do if I take a picture first."

"Fine. Take a picture." Izzy wasn't in a position to argue. She posed for a photograph, then Penny put Monica on loudspeaker.

"You're not the first person to be caught out by a pop-up tent," Monica was saying.

"Yes, pictures are on the way. Now, what do I do with this thing?" Izzy asked.

"You'll need to gather all of the poles together."

"Right. I got that far last time, but then it was all fighting back!" said Izzy.

"Be firm with it. Stand it on end and then firmly spiral it down. It will want to make a large circle, but you must not stand

for that. Make it double up on itself and it will go into a smaller circle."

Izzy tried to follow along, but she hesitated. "Will I break these poles? Surely they are not that flexible?"

"*They really are. Just keep going.*"

Izzy gave the poles another twist and they all dropped into place. "Oh my goodness, they just went into the right shape. It's as if they were deliberately messing about!"

"Very good. Now don't forget we'll want to see those photos." Izzy could hear Monica laughing as she killed the call.

Izzy slid the tent back into its bag. "Well, I think we can be fairly sure that the poles will be flexible enough for what we want."

"Are there enough in that tent for us to finish Remi's hide?" asked Penny.

"Yes. We can finish that quote and you can give him a call."

Penny called Remi and he said that he would pop over to see them.

"Good afternoon," he said as he entered the shop.

"A good day of bird-spotting so far?" asked Penny.

"It is so-so," he said. "I spent ten minutes watching something I thought might be a wading bird but which turned out to be a piece of paper from the fish and chip shop. I see a lot of scarecrows in the town."

"Scarecrow festival this weekend," said Izzy. "The local chamber of commerce has organised it along with the board of trustees for the castle. It's hopefully going to bring a lot of people to the town when we have the scarecrow walk."

"Do the scarecrows walk?" Remi looked confused.

"It's really just a walk around the castle with scarecrows to look at. Guests pay an entry fee and vote on their favourite scarecrow. We should get extra visitors to the town and castle this weekend, which is good for everyone."

"It sounds delightful. Now, you have news about the bird hide, yes?" He gave a delicious waggle of his eyebrows. He looked much more animated than when Penny had first met him. She was pleased that their joint project seemed to excite him.

Izzy slid some paper over to show him the design. "This is how we see it working. A wide collar that supports the calash, and a couple of drawstrings to make it go up and down. We have sourced materials which can be available tomorrow by overnight delivery. The cost is shown at the bottom here."

He studied the paper, then looked between Izzy and Penny. "If you can really do this then I definitely want to buy it from you. Make it happen, please."

"We will!" beamed Penny. "We will order that fabric straightaway. I think we are all looking forward to seeing this come together."

Izzy went to make them all a celebratory cup of tea and Penny turned towards Remi. "What are your birdwatching plans for the rest of your stay?"

"I have more time to spend on the mere. I would very much like to track down the white-tailed lapwing."

"Have you never seen one then?"

"Oh, I have seen them many times on the continent, but they are extremely unusual in England," said Remi.

"Huh." Penny considered that for a moment. "So, the thrill is to see it in a place where it's not expected?"

"Yes it is."

Penny tried to understand. "Is it – I am not sure that this works, but I want to understand – is it perhaps a little bit like when you hear a favourite song on the radio, which is much more exciting than if you just play if for yourself?"

"I think that it's very much like that," said Remi with a nod. "Or perhaps it's like unexpectedly meeting someone special in an unexpected place. Like a sewing shop."

Penny's breath caught in her throat but then Izzy clattered down the stairs with the tea and the moment passed.

14

Much of the rest of the afternoon was taken up with Izzy deconstructing the explosive pop-up tent, while Penny tried to avoid getting poked in the eye by a succession of springy tent poles.

By close of day, there were half a dozen super-thin and super-flexible tent poles on the floor, and a significant pile of cut away fabric.

"What are we going to do with all that old tent material?" said Penny.

"I thought I might use it as a sail to make my bike go faster," said Izzy, holding up the largest section. "If I catch the wind right, I'll be home in no time."

Penny took it off her. "If this thing caught the wind you might get lifted up like Mary Poppins and blown into the North Sea, or all the way across to Europe."

"Ah, to Belgium, the land of waffles, chips, and dreamy-eyed ornithologists," said Izzy with a silly expression for Penny.

"Get away with you," said Penny. "It's home time."

"Tuesday. Rodgers and Hammerstein night," said Izzy.

Penny had already been introduced to Rodgers and Hammerstein nights at her Aunt Pat and Uncle Teddy's house. Izzy's parents enjoyed lively evenings of creating music, and Izzy was already gearing up for a night of Pat's cooking and Teddy's exuberant music.

"We're doing South Pacific this evening," said Izzy.

"Really?"

"A bit of *I'm Gonna Wash That Man Right Outa My Hair*. Fun stuff."

Izzy left. Penny had minimal tidying up to do before she could call herself done for the day. She ate a light dinner and waited for the day's heat to dissipate a little before taking Monty on his evening walk.

She didn't go down to the mere, despite the obvious attractions. If Remi was trying to do a spot of vital bird-watching while it was still light, she didn't want to be the one to disturb him again.

Instead, they walked up the hill to the castle, sticking to the shady side of the street. Lickety Splits, the ice cream shop on the corner opposite the castle entrance, was still doing decent business even as the sun was setting. Penny promised herself a cone on the way back for dessert.

Just over the bridge to the castle, Aubrey Jones was packing equipment away in the back of his decorator's van. "Evening, Penny," he said. "Evening, Monty."

Monty jumped and bounded. The little dog was not

always fond of tall men, but he had nothing but excited yips and licks for Aubrey.

"Still helping set up the bunting?" said Penny.

"Oh, that's done now," he said. "Made a little bit tricky because the police sealed off that section of the walkway."

Penny couldn't help but think about the figures she'd seen among the crenelations in Remi's photo.

"Can you help me understand something?" she said.

"It's not usually the case that Thicko Jones gets asked to help intelligent women to understand things," he smiled.

"No one could ever call you thick," she said.

"You don't go out with a super-qualified doctor," he reminded her.

"You're one of the cleverest men I know."

He scoffed. "How do you reckon that?"

She shrugged. "You're happy. You're almost always happy, and you are always kind. And if half of the point of life is to be happy and the other half is being kind to others then you're succeeding better than most of us. Therefore…"

"I must be amazingly clever." He nodded in amused agreement. "How can Big-Brain Jones help you, now that you've buttered me up with compliments?"

She pointed to the open castle gate. "Can you just help me understand what happened yesterday."

"With Eve Bennefer? Yes, it's sad. It's played on my mind a bit, too."

They wandered through the gate. Penny could see that much of the structure for the scarecrow festival was now in place. There were cordoned off areas for the scarecrow displays and a couple of the marquee tents were up. The scarecrows themselves would be put in position towards the end of the week.

"When Monty and I came into the castle yesterday," she said, pointing to the battlements, "you were up there."

"Er, yes," said Aubrey.

"And Monica was over there." Her finger swung slightly less than ninety degrees to the left.

"I believe she was."

"And the woman, Eve, must have fallen from..."

Aubrey pointed. "Must have been there. There's the remains of the tower. When you're stood by the wall there, you can't be seen directly from either side."

"And the stairs...?"

Aubrey stroked his chin. "There's a set: there and there."

"Right," said Penny. "So, if she wanted to come down again, she'd either have to have come past you or Monica."

"But she didn't," said Aubrey in the tone of someone pointing out the painfully obvious. "She fell."

"But I mean, going up, she would have passed one of you because—" she swept her hand from left to right "—it's stairs. Monica ... tower ... you ... stairs."

"She would have had to come past us," he said. "But I was only up there a few minutes before she ... she jumped. She could have been exploring the castle – gone up there before I went up to do the bunting and already been there for those few minutes before the accident." Aubrey gave her a serious look. "What's bothering you, Penny?"

Penny thought about the camera photo and the two figures. "And you didn't meet her?"

"Eve? No. I'd seen her that morning in the house, but on the castle wall? No. Not at all."

No one had come past either Aubrey or Monica, and neither said they were the figure on the wall next to Eve. There was a time gap of several minutes between the timestamped photograph and the time of Penny's call to the emergency services. It was possible someone had been up there and then slipped away before Aubrey went up onto the wall, but...

"Do you believe in ghosts?" she said.

Aubrey was torn between smiles and frowns. "Are you being haunted?"

She laughed and shook her head. "Izzy's crazy ideas are getting in my head. She was suggesting Pageant House was cursed."

Aubrey's nose twitched and the half-smile disappeared. "Old houses make noises."

"Yes?"

"And you get used to that."

"Yes?"

He nodded. "I spent a lot of time in Pageant House, lugging furniture about and painting the walls behind."

"Uh-huh."

He looked at her directly. "That house makes *a lot* of noises."

"Oh."

He shrugged and the smile was back. "Maybe it's bats in the attic."

"Maybe."

As Penny walked with Monty back down the castle drive

to the main street, she looked across Castle Meadows at Pageant House. The Suffolk pink high walls of the house glowed a deeper colour in the summer sunset. The curtains in the upper storey windows of the house had not been drawn and light played off the dark panes, shifting as she walked.

She stopped at the bend in the road. The ice cream shop had finally shut for the evening. Penny saw a car parked in the short driveway of Pageant House, a sporty little German car, and her attention was immediately drawn to the scratch marks on its rear bumper. She went over and knelt to inspect it. The scratches were long, and in the grooves were smears of paint that she was prepared to bet exactly matched the paintwork on Monica's Land Rover.

"Well, well, well," she said. "What do we think to that, Monty?"

Monty didn't have any comments to that, so they walked home and snuggled together to watch Fred Astaire and Ginger Rogers in *Top Hat*.

15

Izzy had moved out of her parents' house to live with Marcin several months ago, but she popped in to see them at least once a week. Her mum had promised her some home-grown produce from the garden, so Izzy cycled over to their house so she could transport it home in her basket.

"Would you like an oregano scone with spread?" called her mother from the kitchen as Izzy parked her bike.

"I think so," Izzy said, wondering why scones needed oregano.

"I'm trying all of the herbs in scones as an experiment, to see which one works best," said her mum Pat, giving Izzy a hug.

"Blooming coriander scones," said Teddy, her father coming through from the lounge and shuddering theatrically. "Nobody needs a shock like that in their lives."

"You brought that upon yourself by taking one before I told you what they were," said Pat with a smile.

Izzy missed the easy back and forth of her parents. It was as much a part of her upbringing as the family music nights. She had suggested to Marcin that the two of them should join in with one, but it hadn't happened yet.

"Have you got a front runner yet?" Izzy asked. "Obviously it's not coriander."

"Everyone liked the rosemary," said Pat. "I'm thinking of trying geraniums next."

"Whoa!" said Izzy. "Geraniums are not herbs."

"I said that, but she's on a roll now. There's no stopping her," said Teddy.

"I'll pop some on a plate and bring them through," said Pat. "Show Izzy your scarecrow."

Izzy followed her dad in to the lounge.

"It had to be done, didn't it?" said Teddy.

The scarecrow dominated the wall and was dressed in an Elvis suit.

"It's the suit I made for your tribute act!" said Izzy. That outfit had required some unusual materials and specialist touches to complete the cape and the zipper. She wasn't sure how she felt about it being used for the scarecrow festival.

"I know. It's very precious, and I've told that Stuart Dinktrout that he'd better take good care of it, as I don't want any damage. He told me that safety and security are paramount." Izzy laughed as her dad did a passable Stuart Dinktrout voice, capturing the man's smooth pomposity with ease.

"Fair enough. Stuart needs the festival to be a success."

She took a closer look at Elvis's head. "What's his face made from?"

"I found a tub of putty in the shed that was well past its best. I thought I would put it to good use."

"Riiiight. That explains the funny smell."

Pat brought in the scones. "Looks good doesn't it? Your dad doesn't have a gig until after the festival ends, so the costume won't be needed. Makes sense to use what we have, eh?"

Izzy bit into a scone, curious to know how it would taste. "Oh yum!" The oregano gave it a fascinating and fragrant depth. It was still warm from the oven and Izzy thought it was one of the nicest things she'd tasted for a while. "You will have to let me know when you try another herb, I need to be part of this experiment."

"Even geranium?"

"Yes, even geranium."

"Now," said Teddy, "are you staying for Rodgers and Hammerstein night?"

"I've been humming *Some Enchanted Evening* all day," said Izzy.

"That's my girl!" Ted cackled. "Right, you sit tight with your scone and I'll get out the instruments. We need to crank it up to eleven tonight. Mrs Dooley next door's got some new hearing aids and we'd like to give her a bit of a show."

16

On Monty's early morning walk the next day, Penny decided to do a brief tour of the other shops, to see whether there were obvious signs of everyone entering the scarecrow competition. It was well before opening time, so she was limited to peering in through the windows.

Some shops had completed a scarecrow already and displayed it. There were charity shop scarecrows showcasing some of the clothes that had been donated, so they wore quirky vintage outfits. The hardware shop made Penny laugh out loud with their scarecrow: each part of the scarecrow's body was made from flowerpots. Huge ones for the body and smaller ones for the arms and legs. There was a helpful placard at the side which showed an old children's television show called *The Flowerpot Men,* which had provided the inspiration.

"Competition is fierce, Monty," she whispered as they headed back to Cozy Craft.

The shop next door to Cozy Craft was Dougal Thumbskill's games and jigsaw shop. Penny was not surprised to discover he had not entered into the scarecrow spirit. Dougal loved Framlingham with a self-confessed passion, but he would only show his civic pride in his own quiet and idiosyncratic way. Earlier in the year, every shop in the town had put up bright and colourful Easter displays – apart from Dougal. And yet when she'd questioned him about the fact several weeks later, he pointed to the Vietnam War era wargaming diorama on display and said, "It's the 1972 Easter Offensive."

Penny inspected the window for signs of anything obliquely related to scarecrows but could find nothing. What she did spot was a scale model of Framlingham Castle, complete with moulded moat and vegetation formed from that prickly green fuzz she remembered her paternal granddad using to simulate bushes on his model railway.

It was not yet opening time, but she could see Dougal moving near the counter. She rapped on the door and tried the handle. It was open.

"We're not open yet," Dougal Thumbskill said firmly. His shop had been a fixture in the town for many years, but he'd never developed anything resembling customer service.

"I'm not a customer and I need to ask you something."

"Is it can you bring your dog into my shop? The answer is no."

Penny tried to shuffle Monty behind her. "No. I wanted to ask if that model of Fram Castle is accurate?"

"Of course. A one to one-eighty scale model. Accurate to the nearest inch."

"Stairs and everything?"

"Arrow slits, crenulations and doors."

"Excellent," she said. "Can I borrow it?"

The man's expression was more scowl that frown. "That's not for sale. Not unless you've got a thousand pounds in your back pocket."

"I don't want to buy it, Dougal. I want to borrow it."

"It's not a doll's house, you know."

Penny straightened up to her full height and gave Dougal a fixed, meaningful stare. He wasn't the kind of man who enjoyed making eye contact with people and he cleared his throat nervously.

"Did you just assume that a woman with an interest in castles was secretly in search of a doll's house?" she said.

"I'm just saying—"

"Oh, I heard what you said, Dougal," she said, keeping her voice low and calm. "I asked you something nicely and your response was frankly offensive."

"Don't you be getting all PC on me, Miss Slipper—"

"How long have we been friends, Dougal?"

"Are we friends? I didn't think—"

"Neighbours, Dougal. Business neighbours who look out for each other."

"I suppose it's—"

"Years, Dougal. It would be measured in years. I've just come in to ask you a favour and I'd be willing to donate some money to your favourite charity in exchange for that favour."

"Oh, well, since you put it like that—"

"And I promise I will have it back in exactly the same condition that I took it."

"I mean that seems perfectly—"

"Reasonable? Yes. It does."

With only a little awkwardness, Penny bent down and picked up the castle from the table in front of the window. The model, mounted on a thin wooden board, was actually quite weighty. "You'll get the door, Dougal?" she said.

Dougal scooted round and opened the shop door for her. She slid out sideways, the big model against her chest.

"Thank you!" she called as she tottered down to the front door of Cozy Craft. It took her a few awkward moments to get the door open and the model inside. She put it down on the counter with a huff and looked at her dog.

"Now, Monty, I want you to understand that I may appear to have used fake indignation to bully silly chauvinist Dougal into giving me his castle, but please be assured that I'm not in the habit of using my gender as a weapon to get what I want."

Monty seemed entirely uninterested in the matter.

"I'm just saying we won't tell Izzy what I did," said Penny.

"Won't tell Izzy what?" said Izzy, coming in from the back room.

"Oh, you're here," said Penny surprised.

"I'm often here," said Izzy. "I thought you might have noticed by now." She looked at the castle. "There's something different here, but I can't work out what it is. Ah—!" She reached behind the castle and pulled out a cardboard box. "Camouflage patterned nylon. Courier brought it while you were out."

"We're making our scarecrow today, aren't we?" said Penny.

"Priorities," said Izzy, relishing being the sensible one for a moment. "We have a rush job on the bird hide. We have the nylon now, so it's bird hide time!"

"Then scarecrow."

"Sure."

"And I have to show the you the castle."

Izzy gave the model castle an uncertain look. "And, yes, obviously. The castle."

"This all sounds like a chance to work on our time management," said Penny. "If we move forward with the bird hide project and the scarecrow project at the same time, then we can save ourselves some heartache further down the line."

Izzy looked unconvinced.

"We can break it up into time slices. Let's say we spend half an hour now brainstorming scarecrow construction. How would that be?"

"That will be fine."

"Let's start with the basics," said Penny. "What will we use for the scarecrow's body and head?"

Izzy waved her arms at the table in front of the shop. "We are literally selling scarecrow kits! We have all those broom stales and mangelwurzels, so we have the basics covered."

"I know you just like saying 'mangelwurzels'. But is it just too obvious to use those things? If we make our scarecrow from the same basis as everyone else's, do we lose an opportunity to set ourselves apart?"

"There are only so many things that are the right size and

shape to be a scarecrow head," said Izzy. "We could go to all the trouble of finding something different, like a watermelon, and then discover it gives us no real advantage."

"What about the brooms— Hang on, why do you keep calling it a broom stale? Surely it's a broomstick?" Penny said.

"Nope. A broomstick is the whole thing. The stale is the handle."

"I have never heard it called that before."

"I might do a word nerd column about it," said Izzy. She had an occasional column in the Frambeat Gazette. "It is definitely the correct word, and it's possibly the essence of what makes a scarecrow."

"We could use a mannequin instead," said Penny.

"But is it still a scarecrow if you do that?" asked Izzy, with an expansive gesture.

Penny thought about that and sighed. "I see what you're doing. If we try to imagine the thought processes of the judges, they are bound to have some sort of criteria that measures whether an entry is sufficiently scarecrow-like."

"Yes, exactly that."

"Hm. I wonder then if we also need to hand-make as much as we can?" Penny said. "It is our thing, after all."

"There's a fun idea in what you say – like what if every part of our Frida scarecrow was hand-made by us or by things we have re-used."

"I think that embroidered jacket we got from the charity shop has got a Mexican feel to it."

"You want to deconstruct that beautiful jacket for a scarecrow?"

"I might wear it a bit today before we put it on the scarecrow. But re-using and recycling is always a good thing."

"Ooh, we'd be sure to score well for that. Nice idea."

"Good, we can do that." Penny clapped her hands. "What shall we make her hair from?"

They both thought for a long moment. "A yarn wig, I think," said Izzy eventually. "The yarn can come from something old. I'll ask at the charity shop, see if we can get some woollens from the rag bin so we can unravel them. We construct the wig onto something like an old pair of tights."

"We are going to be busy," said Penny.

"Very busy."

17

Izzy decided to tackle the tent poles for Remi's hide while it was early.

"Hey Penny, there must be something useful we could make with the tent fabric afterwards," she called. "What do you think?"

"I bet there is enough there for a kids' workshop," said Penny. "They could make little drawstring bags for their swimming gear."

"That is actual genius!" Izzy picked up one of the poles. "I think I might mark up where I want to cut these, then see if I can persuade Aubrey to bring a saw over and make the cuts."

Penny leaned over to watch. "They are quite long now they've come out of the tent, Better put them somewhere so we don't trip ourselves up!"

"Yes, will do." Izzy put some tape around the places where she wanted them cut, then coiled the poles into a large circle so she could put them out of the way, upstairs. She had to tie them with cotton tape to keep them from uncoiling.

Next she sent Aubrey a text.

I have a small job that needs a saw, if you're passing. It's worth a cake & a cuppa, I reckon.

In this heat, I'd rather have an ice-lolly! he replied almost instantly.

"Aubrey's coming to help cut the poles," said Izzy. "Says he'll do it for an ice cream."

"That man thinks with his stomach," said Penny.

"Don't all of them?"

Penny scuttled round the counter. "I'll go get the ice creams."

"You sure?"

"You're the one who's laid out a tent pole death trap on the floor. You can deal with the customers if they come in." She grabbed the flowery embroidered jacket on her way out.

"Lolly for Aubrey," said Izzy.

Monty looked up from his basket, but didn't seem inclined to go for a walk in the heat.

"I'll get you a doggy ice cream," Penny assured him.

"They do dog ice creams?" said Izzy.

"I believe they do."

"Wonders will never cease."

18

Penny walked swiftly up to Lickety Splits. The sun was not yet high in the sky and the day had to reach its hottest point. Even so the weather did not require a jacket, but she wanted to wear the colourful garment before deciding if it should be sacrificed for a Frida Kahlo scarecrow. The flowers on the lapels popped with vibrancy. It was perhaps a little tight at the shoulders and short in the arms, but such things were bearable.

We waved at Timmy and Old McGillicuddy as the man and his dog tottered down past the church to the market place. Penny crossed over to Lickety Splits on the corner, pausing momentarily to look at the dark windows of Pageant House. Could she tell just by looking at it that the occupant was dead, no longer present? Had the life visibly departed from the house along with Eve Bennefer? The light shifted at one of the closed upstairs curtains as though trying to refute Penny's thought.

She put it from her mind and went into the ice cream parlour.

"Soya cappuccino with sprinkles and a hazelnut shot coming right up," said the woman behind the counter.

"Pardon?" said Penny.

The woman in the pink stripey apron looked at Penny afresh. "Sorry. Don't know where my mind was. Thought you were another regular. What can I get you?"

Penny ordered ice creams, lollies, and a little tub of banana and peanut dog ice cream for Monty, then wandered back to Cozy Craft. Aubrey was already inside when Penny entered.

He waggled the saw in his hand. "I'm here to cut things in exchange for a lolly!"

Penny passed him his ice-lolly while Izzy gathered the poles. Monty gleefully licked and chased round his pot of doggy ice cream at their feet.

"Here, it's this," said Izzy, holding up the coiled tent pole to show Aubrey. "I think it's fibreglass. I need it cutting where the tape marks are."

"Doesn't seem much of a problem," he said. "Lolly first, then cutting, eh?"

Penny licked her chocolate and marshmallow ice cream cone. "Maybe this is time to show you the castle," she said, drawing them over to the counter.

"Impressive model," said Aubrey.

"She didn't make it," said Izzy. "Stole it from Thumbskill's shop – though I'm not sure why."

"Because I need your help solving a conundrum," said Penny. "This is Framlingham Castle."

"Yes, it is," agreed Izzy.

Penny selected a cotton reel from the display and put it on the battlement wall. "This is where Eve Bennefer fell from."

"Oh, right," said Izzy. "This is a serious conundrum, then."

"Here's me, walking Monty," said Penny putting another cotton reel down.

Monty looked up at the sound of his name. He had chase-licked the ice cream tub all around the shop and currently had it cornered against the window display.

"This is Aubrey on the wall here, and this is Monica here."

"When the woman screamed and fell?" said Aubrey. "I was more here." He moved his cotton reel half an inch.

"Note how on both sides, Monica and Aubrey are between Eve and the stairs. Stairs to the left and to the right, blocked by Monica and Aubrey. No one could get to her or from her, from anywhere in the castle, without going past one of you."

"Correct," said Aubrey. "We didn't even know she was there."

"I thought it was a suicide," said Izzy. "Or an accident. She could have been up there for ages. No would have needed to come past Aubrey or Monica."

"Except," said Penny. "Remi took a photo at six fourteen p.m. which shows two people up on the battlements. And seven minutes later, I was calling the emergency services."

"Who's Remi?" said Aubrey.

"He's a Belgian bird-watcher on the mere. Looking for a white-tailed lapwing."

"He might have his eye on Penny too," suggested Izzy.

"Stay focussed," Penny tutted. "Seven minutes from photo to phone call. Someone was with Eve in that time."

"You suspect foul play?" said Aubrey.

Penny couldn't tell if he was joking. 'Foul play' was such an odd phrase that it made her think. "I don't know what I suspect. What I do think is that a wealthy woman who can afford to buy a house for cash and has just arranged to have it redecorated, doesn't sound like the kind of person who would kill themselves. And if there was someone with her, however innocently, why have they not come forward since?"

"As I said before," said Aubrey, "I was up there only a few minutes before she fell. That photo…? There's a window of time where the person could have come down."

Penny shook her head. "If they were in the castle at all, why didn't Frank or Stuart see him or her? They were stood near the only gateway into the castle. Someone can't have been up on the battlements seven minutes before Eve died and have got past them. Could they?"

Izzy stroked her chin, clearly doing her best to look deep in thought. "You think this person pushed her?"

Penny shrugged. "Maybe. I don't know. I'll take any explanation."

"Apart from it being Black Boots the ghost?"

"Yes, apart from that."

Izzy moved her hands over the model. "Let's say Aubrey got into position at six eighteen or something. Just for argument's sake. Remi took his photo at six fourteen and, yes, there are two figures standing there. Six eighteen and Aubrey is blocking the stairs. Six twenty one, Eve is dead and you're on the phone to the ambulance. That's our timeline."

"Yes," said Penny.

"Maybe the other person was still up there after you came rushing down to Eve."

That seemed to be blindingly obvious for an instant before Penny remembered. "After she fell, Aubrey came to the spot where Eve had been standing to look down."

"That's right," said Aubrey. "There was no one there."

"So, our figure came down the stairs between six fourteen and six eighteen or whatever time. A small window of opportunity. But in those few short minutes, they came down."

"But didn't go past Stuart or Frank," Penny sighed.

"It is indeed a conundrum," said Aubrey, then hummed to himself. "Or…"

"Or what?"

"Look here." He ran his fingers along the inside of the castle wall. "There is another level here, right, between the ground and the top. Inside the wall."

"Yes."

"You'd still need to come past me or Monica to get to it, but look—" he rotated the model "—there's a window here."

"A narrow one," said Penny.

"None of us saw Eve fall. None of us knew she was even up there."

"And?"

"What if we only assumed she'd fallen from the top when, in fact, she'd fallen from a window further down?"

Penny wanted to instantly disagree but the idea had some merit.

"Maybe she was never up there," said Aubrey.

"But the photo..."

"Yeah, about that," he said. "You think we can trust the timings on that? The photographer's Belgian, you say?"

"Are Belgians notoriously bad timekeepers?" said Izzy.

"The date stamp on his camera. What if it was set to Belgian time?"

Penny frowned. "It was an hour out?"

"You say the photo was stamped as six fourteen. What if he actually took it at five fourteen or seven fourteen? I don't know what the time is in Belgium right now."

"Oh, that's quite clever," said Izzy.

Aubrey sucked the last of his lolly off the stick. "I like you two. You keep telling me how clever I am."

"We still haven't solved this puzzle," said Penny.

"Yes, especially since we're *supposed* to be making bird-watching calashes and scarecrows," said Izzy pointedly.

"Back to work then," said Aubrey and turned his attention to the tent poles. "Let me see."

He untied the cotton tape holding the pole in a circle. Penny opened her mouth to warn him of the pole's unpredictable tendencies, but she was too late. It whipped out of Aubrey's grasp and smacked him across the cheek as it sprang into its straightened form.

"Good grief!" Aubrey put a hand to his cheek and stared at the pole. "That really smarts!"

Izzy was distraught. "I am so very sorry, Aubrey, I should have warned you what it's like. Let me see, has it cut you?"

He took his hand away from his face. It wasn't cut, but there was a livid red weal across his cheek.

"No blood. Sit down though, that looks very sore," said Izzy.

"What on earth will Denise say if we hurt Aubrey?" said Penny.

"These tent poles are a proper menace."

"That they are," said Aubrey. "I look forward to cutting them up. I *will* have my revenge."

"You should get that seen to," said Penny, looking at Aubrey's cheek.

"If only I knew a doctor, eh?" said Aubrey with a smile.

19

Once Aubrey was done, Izzy had the right lengths of pole she needed for the calash, along with some waterproof camouflage fabric for the hood and the short poncho which would sit over Remi's shoulders. She had selected cotton for the inside of the neck, so that it would be more comfortable where it tied in place.

Izzy had found a handful of people on the internet who had constructed a calash for historical re-enactments, and others who had studied the construction of originals. It had been a fascinating piece of research, although these examples were mostly made from silk or other era-appropriate fabric.

She laid out her materials on the cutting table and cut out a large rectangle for the hood.

Penny came over to look. "I never asked you if you had any plans to make a toile."

"Yeah, I thought about that, as it's such an unknown

quantity," said Izzy. "But it will either work or it won't. It's not really a question of fit."

"True," said Penny. "I am quite fascinated to see how it will look. So, you're going to create channels for the poles, yes?"

"I am," said Izzy. "I will make a sandwich between the outer fabric and the lining, then it's just machine stitching in straight lines."

After sewing the channels, she added pleats at the neck edge, then inserted the poles. Some were longer than others, which would give the calash its shape, narrowing at the front and back.

It was currently flat, and Izzy experimented with bending it into the curved shape that would be needed. "Oh crikey."

"What's up?" asked Penny raising her head.

"I'm starting to think that maybe tent poles are not the right choice for this," said Izzy. "We just want something to maintain a gentle rigid curve."

"A pop up tent does that."

"But that is so much bigger. These short lengths of tent pole take some serious strength to bend them."

Izzy demonstrated by putting the flat construction across the arms of a chair and lowering herself to sit on top. "See? They only bend slightly under my weight!"

"We could find something heavier," said Penny, casting around the shop for something.

"But picture the scene. We need to sew it onto the collar under all that tension. Even if we managed to fasten it, what would happen if it came loose?"

"Ooh, yes. It would be like a weapon."

"Too dangerous. I need to find some cane that I can form into a bent shape. Although one day I might come back to the idea of a weaponised hat."

"For Carmella maybe?"

"Wash out your mouth!" said Izzy in mock horror.

Penny closed her eyes with the effort of remembering something. "Those upholstery supplies that we put in a box, do you remember them?"

"Yes," said Izzy. "Nana Lem said not to get rid of them as they would come in handy when we least expected it."

"What was that stuff coiled up in there? It was reeds or something."

They dug out the reeds and unravelled some.

"This could work," said Izzy.

She replaced the lengths of tent pole with reeds, which already had a curve from being coiled up. The calash started to take on shape, even before Izzy brought the ends together onto the neck band.

"Time to join it onto the neck piece."

Penny came to watch, and also to provide an extra pair of hands, as Izzy worked to sew the hood shape by hand onto the neck piece.

"Well, it's certainly shaping up!" said Izzy, sitting back once they had it secured onto the neck.

"I love it!" said Penny. "What an interesting form it's making. It reminds me of those covered wagons in Western films. What happens at the back here?"

Izzy waved a hand over the gap. "I will sew that up. I made some gathering stitches while it was still flat, and it should come together without any bother. The front is open, but I think I might add something like a veil, in case Remi wants to obscure his face."

Penny held the calash so that Izzy could try it on over her head.

"I'll need neck ties at the front to keep it steady. I was worried it might drag backwards when it's folded down, but it seems fine. Nobody wants to be strangled by their headwear."

"And you're hanging a poncho thing from the bottom of the neck piece?" asked Penny.

"Yes, that will keep Remi dry and camouflaged."

Izzy closed up the back panel and moved onto the poncho. When it was all together, she put it on and approached Penny. "What do you think?"

"I think you look like a Pride and Prejudice cosplayer who is also a mercenary on the side. It's amazing!"

"Help me figure out how the face part should work. A veil like you'd have on a fascinator would be too much, I think."

"What fabric choices do we have? Some sort of green mesh is what we need – and you could have a piece on either side, like curtains."

"Green mesh," Izzy looked around. "Not sure we have anything like that."

"You have that string bag which you get fruit and veg in," said Penny. "That is made from green mesh, in a lovely soft cotton."

"Are you suggesting that I sacrifice my shopping bag because it would make the perfect finishing touch to this project?" laughed Izzy.

"Yep."

"Absolutely. I will get it now."

Izzy draped the soft green mesh at the front opening of the calash and tried out a few different configurations, pinning them in place when she found one that she liked.

"It's nice that there's a finished edge on this bag, around the top. I can use that. A gentle curve on each curtain, and they can overlap a little in the middle. So, I am Remi and I want to take some pictures." She put on the calash and mimed reaching for her camera and poking its lens through the gap. "This will be perfect."

20

"So, shall I let Remi know he should pop in?" asked Penny. She was aiming for a casual tone with her question, but Izzy gave a theatrical wink.

"You definitely should, yes. I'm sure you could persuade him to hang on for a cup of tea as well."

Remi arrived fairly soon after Penny's text. "Hello! I was over in the mere again, so not far away. You have something to show me, yes?"

"We do!" said Izzy. "Maybe you'd like to take a seat and we will put it on you."

Penny had put a chair in front of the mirror, and they ushered him over.

Izzy fetched the calash, and put it on his shoulders. The poncho hung down over his knees, and the calash was fully open, resting at the back of the neck. "I need you to tie this in place, quite firmly," she said, handing him the neck ties.

Remi tied it together and peered at himself in the mirror. "So far so good. I lift up the hood, yes?"

"Go for it."

He reached back and lifted the hoops of the calash, bringing it up over his head. "What a curious garment, and yet, this is a very fine idea. Very fine indeed. And what is this?" He found the mesh curtains and looked at his reflection as he tried them in different arrangements. "This is genius. It obscures my face, and I am sure it will keep flies off, but I can easily see out and take pictures. I take my hat off to the two of you, this is excellent!"

Penny and Izzy grinned at each other.

Remi stood from the chair and strutted back and forth, testing his new garment in different poses. It was slightly comical to see the legs of a normal person with a huge green head. It wasn't far off having a fancy dress grasshopper in the shop, but Penny and Izzy managed to keep straight faces.

"Ring it up!" declared Remi happily. "That is the phrase, yes, when I want to pay?"

Izzy ran it through the till.

"I cannot wait to try it out," said Remi.

"Care for a cup of tea before you go?" Penny suggested.

"No," said Remi, grinning. "I will be straight back to the mere in my new portable hide."

"Yes, yes, of course."

No sooner had he paid than he was rushing out the door.

"He didn't want to stay for a cup of tea, huh?" said Izzy.

"No," said Penny, watching him hurry off down the road.

"Ach, I wouldn't be bothering yourself with a man who doesn't make time for a cup of tea."

"Thanks, Izzy. Does Marcin drink tea?"

"He's more of a coffee person. But he's got dogs. Dogs trump tea."

"Is this how you rate people?" said Penny. "On their tea and pet preferences?"

"It's a deeply complex array of factors."

Penny turned to her cousin. "Nice and speedy work on that calash, by the way."

"Thank you."

"And you turned it around so quickly. I'd like to say that we've earned ourselves a break, but we do need to crack on with our scarecrow."

Izzy rolled her eyes. "You do know I live for crazy projects, don't you? Bring on the scarecrow!"

"Very good! Let's figure out how to divide up the work then. First of all, what will we use for the head?" Penny gave Izzy a significant look, and held her hands in an expectant pose.

"Are you expecting me to say mangelwurzel?"

"I am expecting you to say mangelwurzel."

"Well, yes. While we could use a mangelwurzel – and indeed, I recommend mangelwurzels for scarecrow heads because they are great – I think we should showcase our talents and do something sewn. And thank you for letting me say mangelwurzel more times than is strictly necessary."

"No problem. So what sort of a head shall we do?"

"Some sort of soft sculpture. We could even embroider and appliqué some of the facial features."

"Good. Shall I leave you to make a start on the head, while I see about making some colourful Mexican style clothes?" said Penny, putting her hand on the colourful charity shop jacket.

"Yep!" said Izzy.

~

SEVERAL HOURS LATER, as they were preparing to shut up shop for the day, Penny's phone buzzed. "It's Remi," she said, looking at the number.

"Is it now?" said Izzy. "I wonder why he's calling?"

"Maybe the calash caught the wind and he was blown backwards into the mere."

"Maybe. You could just answer the phone and speak to him."

She was right and Penny knew it. She answered the ringing phone. "Hello?"

"Ah, hello! Hello!" came Remi's excited voice. *"I just had to phone you!"*

"Is everything okay?" said Penny.

"More than okay. This is wonderful. The hood. I like this very much. It worked perfectly. I may have to share my new discovery with the rest of the birdwatching world."

"We're very happy that you like it," said Penny.

"So, so happy. It makes me feel a little guilty that I was sharp with you when we first met."

"Oh, that's noth—"

"And rushed off so soon when I bought the hood."

"No, that's fine."

"So, perhaps I can take you out for dinner to make amends?"

"Oh?" Penny was both delighted and a little taken aback. "Oh!"

She stared at Izzy, wide-eyed. Izzy frowned. *Dinner*, Penny mouthed back to her.

Izzy gave her a double thumbs up and stupidly enthusiastic eyes.

"Dinner?" she said. "Like me and…"

"It was perhaps you who I had specifically offended," he said and she could hear the embarrassed nervousness in his voice now.

"Yes, just me," she said. "That would be lovely, thank you!"

She could hear the smile in his sigh. *"Very good! Tomorrow evening. Is that okay?"*

"That would be great. We'll message to sort details."

"For sure."

She ended the call. "I have a dinner date with Remi. Tomorrow."

"That is lovely."

"Says the woman who judges men on whether they accept or refuse cups of tea."

"Since when have you listened to anything I've said," Izzy smiled.

21

On Thursday morning, Izzy noted down some different options for making the head. She wanted to give it texture and shape, so while calico seemed like a good sturdy base, she thought she might need something else too.

"Hey Penny, do you think it would be a good idea to do Frida Kahlo's famous monobrow using an appliqué of plush fur fabric?" she called.

Penny popped up from behind the counter where she'd been looking for something. "Sometimes I really don't know if you're joking."

"Oh. You think it's a bad idea, then? It's kind of her defining feature. When she did self-portraits she emphasised it a lot."

"It might end up being very disrespectful if we make her look like Colin Farrell," said Penny. "She's well-loved by a lot of people. Why don't you start with something a bit less textured, like felt?"

"Felt it is then." Izzy cut out some shapes and tried them on her own face, to see if they were the right sort of size. She held one in place and went over to Penny. "How does this look?"

Penny pulled a face. "The overall effect is mildly terrifying, but not because it's the wrong shape. More that it's on your face. Why are you doing that?"

"We haven't got a head-shaped thing to try it out on, apart from our own head-shaped heads."

"Well, at the risk of saying something obvious, you could start by making a head," said Penny.

"*Pfft!*" said Izzy, which was her way of saying of course Penny was right, but where was the fun in that?

She cut calico panels to make the basis of a head, then machined them together so that she could stuff it firmly. She found a small length of cardboard tubing from the recycling to form the neck. It was strong enough to hold its shape, and would sit on top of the broom stale when the head was complete. She inserted the tube before using some strong thread to gather and fasten the base of the head around it.

Izzy sat and looked at the head as it sat on its cardboard neck. It was not all that human-shaped yet.

Penny came over to look. "Oh my goodness, I really hope Carmella doesn't come in now."

"You're just saying that because it looks like some sort of weird monster," laughed Izzy. "I plan to give it some shape with stuffed pads." She held up some old tights. "Behold the upcoming nose, cheekbones and chin!"

"Thank goodness. I wasn't sure if this was the finished shape."

Izzy got to work making little pouches, lightly stuffed. First of all she stretched tights right over the head, so there wouldn't be a very obvious change in colour, then she sewed her additional features in place. She embroidered some bright blue eyes and lips onto calico and stitched those in place.

"Oh, this is starting to look really good," said Penny. "How do the eyebrows look now?"

Izzy placed them on the head, with a couple of pins, and they both compared the head with the reference picture on the table.

"If you make some little snips in the middle, so it's not a solid slab of colour, then I think it will look better," said Penny. "What about the wig?"

"There are some balls of dark brown yarn upstairs for making hair," said Izzy. "Then I can tie in a colourful scarf to match the huipil, and sew it all in place."

"I started the huipil," said Penny. "It's such fun because it's a rectangle with a hole in the middle. I can go crazy sewing on embellishments round the neck hole while it's still flat, then make it into a garment at the end. I used plain yellow cotton for the base, and now I'm going to find a couple of bright contrasting braids."

"Not going to desecrate that charity jacket you bought to make it?"

"No. I think it would be wasteful to take apart a perfectly lovely garment for this purpose."

"Quite. We'll be done in an hour or two, then we can

either make a skirt or see if we can find one that will work in the charity shop."

"There's some paperwork we need to fill out for the judges," said Penny, waving a sheet at Izzy. "It describes our entry, in case it's not obvious."

"Why would you make something that is not obvious?" asked Izzy.

"We don't all have the same cultural references, do we? It's in our interest to make it obvious to the judges, so when I find the proper form I will fill it in carefully."

"Paper forms eh? Stuart really doesn't want to move into this century."

Penny shrugged. "He's in charge. I think he enjoys riffling through papers on a clipboard. He's a riffler."

Penny made dissatisfied little noises as she went through the paper. "There is some fine print here."

"What?"

"All valid entries must be delivered to Framlingham castle no later than four p.m. on Friday."

Izzy looked at the clock. "We've still got at least a day."

"We need to work quickly then."

22

The day's work on the scarecrow was hampered somewhat by the number of people coming in for supplies to build their own scarecrows. However, by the close of day, they had the upper body and Mexican huipil tunic complete. They would have to deal with the lower portions and final construction on the last day.

"Oh, you're going out with Remi tonight, aren't you?" said Izzy, as though she had only just remembered, which was not at all the case.

"That is correct," said Penny neutrally.

"What's his surname?"

Penny frowned. "Why? In case he kidnaps me?"

"I'm just asking."

"He did tell me…? De Smoot? De Smut?"

"De Smut?"

"Something like that. I can ask him if you like."

"Do."

"Tonight's meal will be a simple and straightforward thing, just to celebrate a finished project and to make amends for getting off on the wrong foot," said Penny.

"Who are you trying to convince?" said Izzy.

Penny shut and locked the till. "It's not a date is it?"

"Of course it's a date. You two were making goo-goo eyes at each other while I was standing right there."

"Goo-goo eyes? I have no idea what that even looks like! Show me goo-goo eyes."

Izzy pulled a face, making her eyes huge.

"No. That is not a face I ever pulled in my life. That is somewhere on the unlikely scale between 'Bambi' and 'crazed clown'." Penny grinned at the stupidity of it all. "Seriously though, what should I wear?"

"Wear something that looks nice and you will be comfortable in," said Izzy. "Do you have a sense of déjà vu? I feel as though we have trodden this path before. Is it a date? Ooh, what shall I wear?"

Penny gave her a good-natured nudge with an elbow. "I know. With enough practice, maybe I will figure out how to do this."

"I mean, now that you and I are old ladies, we fall out of practice with these things."

"Old ladies, huh?"

Izzy grinned. "You ever spoken to children. They assume everyone over twenty-five is just waiting for death's icy fingers on their shoulder. Why not wear that linen dress you made?"

"You think?"

"It will be hot well into the evening. You just need a wrap or something for your shoulders, if it gets cooler later on."

"Yes, that would be a good choice I think.

Penny wore the linen dress and folded a wrap into her handbag for later. After a final evening walk for Monty and leaving him at the shop (which was only achieved by offering the whiny pooch a dog biscuit to distract him while she shut the door), Penny walked down the road to the Station Hotel where Remi sat waiting by a bench table, idly adding details to a sketch in his book.

He wore a corduroy jacket and a shirt that didn't match over drainpipe jeans and a pair of white-laced plimsolls. It looked like he had dressed in the most formal clothing he had brought with him on his bird-watching holiday.

"Ah, there you are," he said, putting the sketchpad away in his rucksack. "I hope this place is okay. The internet says that Taylor Swift and Ed Sheeran came here once. Is that true?"

"Probably," said Penny.

They ordered drinks and sat opposite each other, enjoying the slight breeze which stirred the air. Remi pointed out birds wheeling high above them in the orange evening sky.

"Swifts. They come all the way from Africa to spend the summer here. A remarkable journey."

Penny smiled. "How are you enjoying Suffolk?" she asked.

Remi seemed to give this considerable thought. "It's very lovely. An interesting mixture of habitats. Heathland, farmland, coastal, and of course some mixed wetland like your beautiful mere."

"It's interesting to hear it described that way."

"How would you describe it?"

It was her turn to think. "I grew up in Suffolk, but left to work in London for a time. And now I see Suffolk as this beautiful place tucked away in a corner of England that no one ever passes through, unless they mean to come here. Far enough away from the hurly-burly—"

"The what? I do not know this phrase."

"Hurly-burly. Far enough away from the city and the noise that it can seem like it's its own quiet idyllic world. Although not far enough away to stop certain wealthy outsiders buying their second homes here."

"Yes. I thought it quite expensive to stay here. Rich London people pushing up the prices?"

"Maybe."

"My accommodation is basic but good. Enough for while I watch the birds."

"It obviously gives you a lot of satisfaction to spot birds," she said.

"Of course." His eyes were alight with excitement. "If we have a subject which we are passionate about, then it is satisfying to expand our experience and knowledge. Is it the same for you with sewing?"

"Yes, it is," said Penny. "It definitely is. I've learned so much since I came here and teamed up with Izzy."

"You work well together?"

"Yes we do. She nudges me outside my comfort zone all the time, which is good. I like to think that I tether her a little, so that we tackle things that are achievable."

Remi laughed at that. "Well, who knew that inventing a new kind of bird hide was achievable?"

Their starters arrived. Penny had barbecued sardines and glanced across at Remi's crab cake salad.

"As much as I love sardines, I am a little envious of your amazing salad. It's like a work of art," she said.

"It is very colourful," he said. "Tell me, what is a sardine? I guess our countries share similar fish stocks, but I don't know this one."

Penny pondered the question. "I don't know. You're right, I don't think I ever heard of sardines swimming around. I wonder if they go by a different name?"

"Is it rude to consult the internet while on a date?" asked Remi, pulling his phone out.

"No ruder than eating sardines on a date," said Penny. She felt her cheeks flush. At least it was out in the open: this was definitely a date. But had she just hinted she might be spoiling any upcoming kisses by eating strongly-flavoured food? This was outrageous flirting by Penny's standards.

Remi didn't notice her discomfort as he searched on his phone. "Interesting. It seems as though sardines are different fish depending on where you live. Here in the UK they are young pilchards, but in other countries they can be other small oily fish."

"Well I never! I must tell Izzy, she loves things like that."

"How odd it is. We give things names based on where we find them and assume they are the same. Often with birds it is the same. Things can be misidentified. Things that are identified as the same can be different. Only recently they have discovered that two identical looking species of plover in China are two species: the Kentish plover and white-faced plover."

"Have they really?" she said politely. "Any luck with finding your white-tailed lapwing yet?"

"No. Not yet. But even I do not find it, I will not be sad."

"Really?"

"Yes. It is..." He pursed his lips. "...*mijn hoed op te hangen*. It is the excuse for the holiday. The white-tailed lapwing is the excuse, but the treasure I find may be something entirely different." And just like that, he placed his hand over hers on the table.

Penny, surprised, drew her hand back at once and immediately regretted it. "Oh, I am sorry," she said and clumsily put her hand on his.

His cheeks blushed and he withdrew his own hand. "I was too ... forward. That was..."

"No, no, no," she said, half taken by the urge to reach across the table, grab his hand back and never let go. "I was just surprised. I don't..." She sighed. "It's been a while."

"How long is a while?" he said, with a small smile.

"Depends what you're counting. There was a man – well, two men. Not at the same time—!" she added rapidly. "But there were options. I took one, and he left almost instantly for New York. Not that I scared him off – at least I don't think I did. But he left."

"And the other man?"

"Is now taken," she said. Fearing she'd left a questioning tone in that statement, firmly added, "Definitely taken."

"Ah."

At that point, the mains arrived. When they were placed and Remi was smoothing a napkin into his lap, he said,

"Birds, and all animals, are driven by an urge to find a mate and to have offspring."

"Er, yes," said Penny, wondering if this was a weird ornithological way of him questioning if she wanted to settle down and have children.

"Mate, offspring, find food, survive. Round and round it goes. We sometimes forget we are not trapped in that same cycle."

"No?"

"No. Because we have these." He tapped the side of his head before picking up his cutlery. "Brains. We can think ahead; we can envisage our futures. We can picture our own inevitable deaths."

"What a cheery thought!" said Penny.

"It is!" he insisted. "We get to think about what it is we really want. We are not tied into just having babies and continuing our genetic family tree. We can decide what we want to achieve in the time we have. Bird-watching, dress-making, teaching physics and chemistry to naughty children."

"Um, that last one...?"

"Oh." He laughed. "I am a school teacher when I am not spotting birds. Petrus und Paulus School in Ostend. Crazy Mr De Smet, the science teacher."

"A teacher. Fantastic."

"So, as humans we are free."

"I bet dating is easier for birds," she said.

"Simpler in their minds perhaps, but no less cruel and difficult."

"Cruel and difficult," she smiled.

"For sure!" He grinned back. "Ritual mating displays. You have great crested grebes on the mere. If I had been here earlier in the year, I would have seen their courtship dances, where their relationship is tested to its very limits."

"Really?"

"It is impressive. First, there is the 'ghostly penguin display'."

"That sounds like something you've just made up," she said.

"Not at all, Penny."

He put down his fork, stood up, and took several steps back. Penny looked around the rear garden where other drinkers and diners sat.

"You ... you're about to show me this courtship dance? The ghost penguin?"

"The ghostly penguin display. Sure. It is where one of the grebes invades the other's personal space from underneath to see how they react." He looked about too. "Am I embarrassing you with this?"

Her instinctive answer was 'yes', but Penny hesitated. If this funny, handsome Belgian wanted to prance about for her entertainment, then why shouldn't she let him. "Not at all," she said, firmly.

"Good! And then I will show you the grebe's weed ceremony."

"Weed ceremony. Looking forward to it," she said, realising she meant it.

23

Izzy was curled up in one corner of the sofa, her sketchpad on her knee. She was idly sketching ideas for some stuffed parrots they could place around their Frida Kahlo scarecrow. She had no real intention of making them, but at the other end of the sofa Marcin was watching a documentary about arctic explorers in which she had no real interest. Two of Marcin's dogs, Wooster and Tibia, were sprawled on the thick rug, snoozing. Their ears pricked up every time a husky howled on the screen, but neither woke.

Izzy knew they didn't have time to make stuffed parrots. She was a little worried they wouldn't actually have time to finish the scarecrow by the cut-off time tomorrow. Would Stuart Dinktrout and Frank Mountjoy be there, judge and castle trustee, closing and locking the castle gate against anyone coming in after four o'clock? Izzy was finding herself wondering if handyman Aubrey had a key to that castle gate when her phone buzzed with a text from the man himself.

This was a surprise, but not much of one. Izzy was a firm believer that the universe spoke to individuals, and that coincidences were just silent nudges from fate.

The text simply said, *Are you free to talk?*

Izzy replied that she was and seconds later her phone rang. Wooster almost looked up from his slumber but didn't quite manage it. Izzy slipped out into the kitchen to answer it, placing a kiss on the top of Marcin's head as she passed him.

"Hello, Aubrey," she said, sitting down at the kitchen table. "I was just thinking about you."

"Were you?"

"I was wondering if you had a key to the castle gate."

"Why would you...? I mean I do, but— Can I go first?" He sounded flustered and unhappy.

"Please do," she said.

"Um. You're an open-minded woman, aren't you?"

"Yes?" said Izzy, who didn't really know how one was meant to answer a question like that.

"I mean, if I tell you something you won't just dismiss it or laugh at me?"

"No."

"Because I can't tell Denise. She's, um, very practically minded. And I know you're a bit more..."

"Bit more...?"

"A bit more receptive to unusual ideas."

Izzy pulled a face at the empty kitchen. "I don't think I've ever had it expressed to me in those exact words before. But, yes. Do go on."

There was a pause, a taking in of breath. *"Do you believe in ghosts, Izzy?"*

It was not a question she'd been expecting. "I don't *not* believe in ghosts," she said.

"Right. Exactly. So you agree there might be something…"

"Have you seen something, Aubrey?"

"Not seen, no. Heard. If I could play my voicemail message back to you over the phone… I don't think I can do it. Is it too late for me to come over and show you?"

"Sure," she said, happy to help and more than a little intrigued. "You want to play me a voicemail?"

"Yes. Except it's from a dead person."

"A dead person?"

"Yes."

"A dead *dead* person?"

"It's Eve Bennefer," said Aubrey. *"It's the woman who fell off the castle wall. She's just phoned me."*

Izzy was not sure what to say to that, but quickly settled on, "Then you must come over at once. I'm very keen to hear it."

24

Penny and Remi walked along College Road. It was a direct route to Remi's accommodation and a somewhat more circuitous route back to Cozy Craft. They had eaten their mains and dessert and Remi had invited her back to his for coffee. She had surprised herself by saying yes.

At some point, he offered her his arm and she felt foolish and child-like at the shiver of pleasure which ran through her as she took it.

His accommodation was a sub-divided house not far from the private school. He gained access via an electronic keypad and led her through to the kitchen.

"Not quite a hostel. Not quite a hotel. There are no staff here at all," he said. "Internet booking, codes for everything. Perhaps this is the future of holiday accommodation."

The kitchen was simplistic but clean. A pair of French windows opened out onto a patio area where a fire pit gently glowed. A slender middle-aged woman sat with her bare feet on the wall around the fire pit and looked out over the long, darkening garden.

"Hello, Becky," called Remi.

The woman, Becky, looked round, her expression shifting, as though she was coming back from a distant, contemplative place.

"Ah. Remi." She saw Penny. "You're new."

Becky had a drawl to her accent. Not a Suffolk accent, but something not a million miles away either.

"I am new. Penny. I'm with Remi." She glanced at him. "I mean, not *with* Remi. I'm just with Remi."

Becky laughed, although there wasn't much humour in her voice. "A successful date then, Remi?"

"Indeed," he said.

"He showed me his ghostly penguin display and weed ceremony," said Penny.

"You've got weed?" said Becky, hopefully.

"Not that kind of weed," he said. "I am making coffee. Want some?"

"Soya cappuccino with sprinkles and a hazelnut shot," she said instantly.

Remi hummed. "Your choices are … cafetière coffee *with* milk or cafetière coffee *without* milk."

"I'll pass," she said.

The woman's words prompted a thought in Penny's mind. "Excuse me. Becky, is it?"

"Yes?"

"Have you ever been up to Lickety Splits ice cream place, near the castle?"

Becky frowned. "Why?"

In the light from both the fire pit and the kitchen, Penny could make out Becky's features. The woman looked nothing like Penny, and yet...

"Do you perhaps own a colourful cotton jacket? Bold colours? Flowers on the lapels?"

"No," said Becky, her frown becoming more intense. "That is a very odd question ... Penny, was it?"

"Yes."

The woman looked at her phone. "I have places to be." She put her feet in some slip-on shoes by the side of the firepit and, with a silent glare for Penny, went inside.

Remi poured hot water into the cafetière.

"Interesting woman," said Penny.

"She has been here as long as me," said Remi. "But she has not travelled as far. A town called Great ... Yarmouth..."

"Norfolk," said Penny.

"Norfolk," he agreed. "Norfolk and Suffolk. The north folk and the south folk, yes?"

"I suppose so. Milk in mine, please."

"And we have a warm pit to sit next to," he said, gesturing.

They settled side by side on wooden deckchairs by the fire pit. There was a pleasant feeling in Penny's chest and it took her a little while to identify it as contentment.

"This has been a very, very nice evening," she said.

"Two 'very's," Remi noted.

"Supremely nice," she said.

"Exceptionally nice," he said.

"Extraordinarily."

He sipped his coffee. "I will soon return to Belgium."

"I know."

He gestured at the sky. "But like our friends the swifts, I am sure to return."

It was a cheesy comment, but she liked it anyway. "Why do they come here?" she asked. "The swifts. They could stay in Africa and save themselves a long journey. Is it too hot for them?"

"It's more to do with using the extra hours of daylight. Migratory birds come here for the longer days so that they can catch enough food to raise their young."

Penny gave a rueful smile. "Making the most of summer, eh? I bet there's a lot we can learn from birds."

25

It was, as Aubrey had indicated, a voicemail from a dead woman.

"Play it again," said Izzy.

Leaning against his van bonnet in the yard outside the farmhouse, he tapped back to replay.

"Mr Jones. Eve Bennefer here. It's Wednesday evening and I'm standing in my hallway and I see that you have not completed the work you promised to have done. I don't pay to have work half complete. Come over as soon as you get this. We clearly have unfinished business." The message clicked and ended.

"Unfinished business," said Aubrey. "That's exactly the kind of thing ghosts say."

Izzy made a range of faces and puffed her cheeks out. "I have to say, I've not spoken to many ghosts. But, yes. And you got that today?"

"Today. An hour ago. She says Wednesday in the message. It's not been stuck in the—" he waved his hands at the air and the unseen telecommunications network "—in the aether for a week or something. She phoned me. A ghost. A ghost! It is a ghost, right?"

She shrugged. "I don't know. I guess! She has phoned you and she's definitely dead. Did you go round to see her?"

His eyes were wide. "Go visit a ghost when they invite you? That sounds like a dangerous thing to do."

It was that peculiar moment in the summer evening when the sky is filled with a bright orange glow from a sun that was just below the horizon, but the land itself is dark, as though sky and earth were separated: one in day and one in night.

"I could come with you," Izzy suggested.

"Go visit her now?

"She did say come at once."

"This is a ghost we're talking about."

"Or there's some other explanation."

Aubrey jiggled as he weighed up the options. "I guess I don't like to leave customers unsatisfied, even if they are dead. Sure."

"Good," Izzy nodded firmly. She went back to the house, poked her head round the kitchen door and called out. "Marcin! Aubrey and I are going to pop out and see a ghost!"

"Okay!" Marcin replied. "Shall I put the kettle on for when you get back?"

"Good idea!" she said and closed the door. "Let's go," she said as she climbed into Aubrey's van.

It was a two minute drive to Pageant House. There was a car in the driveway and another car on the roadside, blocking it in. Aubrey had to drive on a little further to find a parking space.

"Oh, while I remember," he said and reached over to the glove compartment. He took out a big bunch of keys on a ring. He unclipped a large iron one with a pink ribbon on it. "One of two spares I have for the castle gate."

"I was only asking speculatively," said Izzy. "I thought that if Penny and I were late with our scarecrow..."

"Sure, sure," he said. "I trust you. Now, the lock is a bit old so sometimes you have to give a bit of a jiggle, and I mean a real jiggle not a—"

Izzy put her hand on his. "Aubrey, are you doing this with the keys because you're trying to put off going into the house?"

"What? No. What, me? I..." He looked round, staring at Pageant House through his wing mirror. "Seriously, what are we doing?" said Aubrey. "She's dead." It was odd, funny even, to find the big man sounding so nervous.

"We knock at the door and see who answers," said Izzy.

"And if it's a ghost?"

"Then we have a lot of questions to ask it."

He managed a smile. "You see, Denise would have told me to stop being such an idiot by now."

"A wise woman with both feet on the ground," said Izzy, taking the gate key and getting out.

They crunched up the short gravel driveway and, when Aubrey hesitated, Izzy knocked on the door. The door swung in a few inches. The hinges didn't creak, but Izzy thought it was spooky nonetheless.

"I do not like this," said Aubrey.

"It's the countryside," said Izzy. "Lots of people leave their doors unlocked." She pushed it open and stepped inside. "Hellooo! Miss Bennefer? Anyone in?"

There was no reply. The kitchen light was on and there was light in the hallway beyond.

"It's just me and Aubrey!" Izzy called. "We mean you no harm."

There were dust cloths and some of Aubrey's painting gear on the side counters.

"So you didn't get her painting job finished then?"

"She'd gone away while I was doing it, but she returned early and we had that spat and—" Aubrey suddenly gripped her arm. "Did you hear that?"

"Hear what?"

"There was a thumpy, creaky sound."

"I didn't," she said honestly. "Old houses make noises."

"That's what I told Penny. But still…"

Izzy patted his hand. "Listen, there will be a reason for the voicemail. I don't understand it yet, but Eve Bennefer is definitely dead. She fell off a castle wall and broke her neck or whatever. People really don't tend to do much moving around or talking after that."

She walked on into the hallway and came to a sudden stop.

There was a body on the floor. A woman was sprawled at the foot of the sweeping staircase, arms spread, her hair fallen around her. Izzy looked up at the dark staircase and then at the woman.

"Eve?"

"Oh, heck!" said Aubrey.

Izzy rushed forward and knelt beside the woman. She took her wrist. It was warm.

"Hello? Can you hear me? Eve?"

Izzy put her head to the woman's mouth to try and hear for breathing.

"Is she alive?" said Aubrey, quietly.

Izzy started to shake her head. "Call emergency services anyway. I don't ... I just don't understand this."

26

Penny received the text message from Izzy as she was just about to open the door to Cozy Craft and go upstairs to bed.

She took her key out of the door and went straight up Market Hill and round the corner towards Pageant House. There were silent emergency lights reflecting off windows all along Church Street. Two police cars were parked outside, effectively blocking the street.

A policeman stood beside the car with the scraped bumper in the driveway.

"Excuse me," said Penny. "I need to get in there."

The policeman held up his hand to ward her off. "Can you step back, madam. We can't have members of the public coming in here."

He was the second person in a week to call her madam. Would it hurt for people to actually look at other's faces and recognise that she was far more a 'miss' than a 'madam'?

"I just..."

"Step back. Please."

Penny stepped back. The policeman turned his back on her so he could speak into his radio. "So this Audi is registered to Ulrike Merrison? Can you spell that?"

The side door to the house opened. Penny saw Izzy and Aubrey come out onto the driveway in the company of Detective Sergeant Dennis Chang from Woodbridge police station.

Penny waved urgently. "Izzy!"

The policeman whirled on her, irritated. "Madam! I asked you step back."

Penny scowled at him. "It's 'miss' for goodness sake! Look at me. Do I look like an old housewife? Or do you see so many faces they all blur into one?"

The policeman was about to answer when DS Chang called out. "It's okay, Connor. Let her through."

Penny grumpily stepped past him and hurried to Izzy and Aubrey. She took hold of one, then the other, as though trying to squeeze some love and care into each of them. "Are you okay?"

"We were just trying to get to the bottom of the matter," said Detective Chang. "Did you have any part in this, Miss Slipper?"

At least Dennis Chang took the time to remember faces and names. Sadly, his recollection of Penny was perhaps most closely linked to the time last year when a body was found in the upstairs toilet of Cozy Craft.

"Part in what?" she said.

The detective consulted his notepad. "Mr Jones here tells me he received a phone call from Eve Bennefer earlier this evening, asking him to come over. He also tells me that he didn't come here until he had brought along Miss King as a witness."

"As a witness...?" said Aubrey. "What?"

"Wait," said Penny. "Eve Bennefer died on Monday. At the castle. I was there."

"Oh, you were?" He made a note in his pad. "And was that corpse at the castle identified as Eve Bennefer by you, Mr Jones?"

"Yes. I guess," said Aubrey. "I mean, yes, it was. I'd seen her only earlier that day. She'd shouted at me."

"You had an argument?"

Aubrey opened and closed his mouth a couple of times. "I don't argue. She might have had an argument with me, but I didn't. I don't."

"Not so much a man of words but a man of action," said Detective Chang.

"I don't know what you're suggesting."

Dennis Chang looked up at the castle. It was just about visible as a dark silhouette against the night sky. "We have a very peculiar situation here."

"Tell me about it," said Izzy.

"Mr Jones. Aubrey. You were contracted by Miss Eve Bennefer to paint her house."

"Top to bottom," said Aubrey. "She'd just bought it."

"There was an altercation on Monday."

"She'd come back early and hadn't expected me to be there. There was barely any argument."

"But later that day a woman fell to her death from the castle wall. I read the file. You were there."

"I was at the castle."

"On the wall," said Detective Chang pointedly. "Today, you received a voicemail, an angry message, purportedly from Eve Bennefer, telling you to come here. Sometime later, you brought Izzy with you and found a woman dead at the base of the stairs. Her skull is fractured. I'm guessing she fell. Like the woman at the castle."

Even in the poor light, Penny could see how pale Aubrey's face had become. "None of this makes sense," he said.

"On that we agree," said the detective. "I would like you to come to the station with me. We will be interviewing you under caution. Do you understand what that means?"

"You're arresting me?"

"Not yet," said Detective Chang. "Let's just have a nice chat about this at the station and see if we can get to the bottom of this."

Penny watched aghast as the detective led Aubrey to a waiting police car.

27

Friday morning was an unpleasantly subdued affair in the Cozy Craft shop. They still had plenty of work to do on their Frida Kahlo scarecrow, but the shocks of the previous evening seemed to have robbed their fingers of the energy to do any work. The summer's heat was now an oppressive cloth that covered and smothered everything and seemed to press the life out of the world.

"I just can't believe it," said Izzy for the fifth time.

"I don't understand it," said Penny, also for the fifth time.

"How can a woman die twice?"

"Well, she can't," said Penny.

Penny stared numbly at the cloth and thread in front of her. There were thoughts ticking over in her mind, but she was too depressed to grasp at them properly. "Eve Bennefer couldn't have died twice," she said.

"That's what I said."

"I mean she couldn't. Could not. So she didn't."

"I fear you're repeating yourself, cousin."

Penny shook herself. "What I am saying is that if we accept that Eve Bennefer couldn't have died twice, then one of those women was not Eve Bennefer. Okay?"

"Correct."

"So maybe the woman who fell off the castle wall was not Eve Bennefer."

"No," said Izzy. "Aubrey was there, you said. He identified her. He'd been in her house only hours before. He'd spoken to her. He recognised her."

"Okay. Then the woman in the house last night – maybe that wasn't Eve Bennefer."

"Sure," said Izzy. "Then how do we explain the voicemail message. It was definitely sent last night."

"Pre-recorded from before her death?" suggested Penny helplessly.

"She mentioned the day in the message."

"Then maybe it was someone pretending to be her." She recalled the policeman in the driveway. "There is a car parked on the drive of Pageant House…"

"The silver one," said Izzy. "The one that scraped Monica Blowers' Land Rover."

"Yes. I heard the policeman talking to HQ or whatever and he said it was registered to … ooh, what was it? Ulrike! Ulrike Merriman or Merrison. Something like that."

"So, someone else had parked her car on Eve's drive."

"Maybe that woman pretended to be Eve in the voicemail," said Penny. "Did Aubrey recognise the voice as Eve's?"

"He assumed it was her. We're not always good at

recognising voices. She didn't have a local accent. Norfolk or something, I guess."

"Norfolk..." That did ring bells in Penny's mind. "That Norfolk woman. That's what Frank Mountjoy said to me at the castle on the day Eve – or whoever! – died."

Izzy nodded enthusiastically. "Right. Right."

The pieces of the puzzle were there, even if Penny had no idea how they fitted together. Two women. A car. A voicemail. A Norfolk connection.

Another thought came to her, another Norfolk connection. "I need to check something out," she said and went to the other room.

"We need to get on with this scarecrow," said Izzy. "I might have a key to the castle, but I'd rather get our scarecrow handed in before the official deadline."

Penny came back through to the shop, colourful charity jacket in her hand.

"I don't think you'll need that," said Izzy.

"I do. It's vitally important. What flavour ice cream?"

"Pardon? I thought you were checking something out."

"I am. And it involves ice cream."

"Er, raspberry ripple then."

Penny dashed out, clutching the jacket, and hurried up Church Street to Lickety Splits, narrowly avoiding colliding with a family of four coming out with cones and tubs. She apologised and scooted past them into the shop. It was the same woman behind the counter as on previous visits.

"You're in a hurry," she noted.

Penny held up the jacket for the woman to see. "Last time I came in here, I was wearing this."

Penny half expected the woman to give her an odd look or to make a confused comment, but she just nodded and smiled. "I did. Don't see many of them about."

"And you thought I wanted a soya cappuccino with—"

"With sprinkles and a hazelnut shot. I did. Sorry about that."

"No. It's fine. But that's because someone else had that drink. Someone wearing this jacket."

"That's right. You don't see many coats like that. Beautiful thing. Too gaudy for my liking, but nice if you're into that type of thing. Were you actually after something?"

"Oh. Certainly. A raspberry ripple and a mint choc chip."

The woman set to the tubs behind the counter with her metal scoop.

"The person who wore this," said Penny. "She was from Norfolk. Great Yarmouth."

"Was she?"

"You saw her plenty of times if you were memorising her order."

The ice cream woman chuckled. "I have a good memory. But, no, she'd only been coming in for the last week or so. It was every morning. Almost always the first one here. Soya cappuccino and a seat by that window."

"That window?" Penny went to the indicated table and crouched a little to get a seated person's view. The table looked out on to the street with a perfect view of Pageant House, straight across the road. "She sat here, watching that house."

"Or maybe she just liked the view of the castle."

Penny tried to work out what it meant. Becky, who was

staying in the same accommodation as Remi and who, despite what she said, had owned a jacket very much like this, had been coming here every morning to watch Pageant House.

"Was she here on Monday?" said Penny. "The day that woman had the accident at the castle."

"Oh, terrible business. Well, yes. Like I say, every morning. In fact, that was the last time I saw her in here, I think."

"Interesting."

"Is it?" said the woman, holding up two ice cream cones.

Penny smiled politely, paid the woman, and left with the ice creams. She walked quickly back to Cozy Craft, ice creams in hand, the speed of her feet powering the speed of her thoughts. Pieces of the puzzle. Norfolk. A car outside Pageant House. A woman watching from the ice cream parlour. Eve Bennefer, Ulrike Merrison, and this Becky character.

Penny pushed the shop door open with her elbow.

"Oh, I'm glad you're here, I—" Izzy began.

Penny thrust an ice cream at her. "Gotta go. One more thing to check out. Maybe two."

"But I wanted to tell you—"

"I won't be long. Promise."

28

Penny headed out again, licking her melting ice cream to stop it trickling down the cone and over her fingers. She hurried round to College Road and the door of the hostel. There was no doorbell, only the entry keypad. Penny rapped urgently on the door.

There was no response for quite a time and then it was opened. By Remi. "Hello!" he said. "What a surprise!"

She gave him a quizzical look. "Why aren't you out twitching? The sun is up and the birds are about."

He rubbed an eye with the palm of his hand. "I may have had a few more beers than expected last night. A lie-in was needed. You look like you have been up for a while." He looked meaningfully at her ice cream.

"It's been a long night and a busy morning." She didn't want to explain everything about the business at Pageant House and Aubrey being taken away by the police. "First and foremost," she said instead, "I really enjoyed last night."

He smiled. There was such relief in happiness in that smile she momentarily thought about kissing him there and then.

"I didn't embarrass you with my bird impressions?" he said.

"No. Do you do them at every opportunity?"

"I can stop myself if I need to," he said carefully.

"Fair enough."

"And so maybe, if you did not find me so off-putting, and since I have to go back to Belgium on Sunday on my little motorbike and sidecar, maybe you would like to go out with me again tonight."

"Tonight. So soon?"

"You object?"

"No," she said. "I do not. Not at all. We should do that. Strike while the iron's hot. Not that I'm hot. Or you're hot. I mean it *is* hot. But that's not what I mean. I'm babbling."

His smile broadened. "We *make hay while the sun shines*," he said in the slow manner of someone who had learned an English idiom and was pleased to use it.

"Yes! A much better metaphor. We will make hay while indeed the sun does shine." She remembered herself. "I came here for a reason."

"Yes?"

"Becky."

Remi jerked a thumb over his shoulder. "Becky here?"

"Yes. Is she in?"

He stuck out his bottom lip and shrugged. "We can check."

Her door was on the ground floor, not far from the

entrance. Remi knocked politely but firmly. "I didn't hear her come in last night. Not since you asked her peculiar questions about jackets and flowers." He saw the jacket Penny had in her hand. "Is that the one?"

"Her jacket is like this one."

"Wow."

"Wow?"

"I am surprised there are two such jackets like that in the world."

She caught his tone. "You don't like it?"

"I do not judge," he said. "I am a man who has been wearing a camouflaged tent on his head. But that looks like a very, um, unique jacket."

"Perhaps," she said, then the thought expanded in her mind. "Oh, my!"

"Oh, my?"

"A brainwave," she said. "Gotta dash." And because the moment simply took her, she stood on tiptoes and put the tiniest kiss on his lips. "Really gotta dash," she said.

"You taste of mint!" he called out, laughing as she hurried away.

Her cheeks burning with more than summer heat, Penny marched back into town and straight into the Community Change charity shop. Monica Blowers was behind the counter.

"Scarecrow shopping are we?" she asked.

"What makes you think that?" said Penny, somewhat out of breath.

"It's what everyone's been doing today. Final day. Hats have been especially popular!"

"I don't need a hat – although maybe I will look for a scarf. What we actually need is a skirt. But that's not really why I'm here."

"Oh?"

"Ulrike Merrison," said Penny. "Ever heard of her?"

"Who?"

"Ulrike Merrison."

"Never heard of her."

"She drives a silver Audi. She's the one who dinged your Land Rover."

Monica instantly had a pen in her hand, hovering over little pad of post-its. "Ulrike, you say. Can you spell that?"

"No, I can't. You'd have to ask the police. Never met her?"

"Never heard the name."

"Fair enough. Her car is at Pageant House."

"The woman who died?"

"No, that's Eve. Possibly. Someone is dead. Two someones." Penny held up the jacket. "Actual reason I'm here. I bought this from you."

"You did. Want to re-donate it?"

"I need to know how you got it."

Monica looked baffled. "The usual. Is there any other way?"

"It was dropped off here as a donation. On Tuesday you said it had just come in that day."

"I probably did."

"Is there any chance it was dumped among the other donations people leave on your doorstep overnight?"

"There's every chance."

"Like loose, on the top?"

"Not like that. Everything bagged up. I can't recall what bag it was in, but there were no loose items. What's this all about?"

Penny couldn't explain. There were too many pieces to the puzzle, but somehow she instinctively felt it would make sense when put together. "You've been very helpful."

"Glad to hear it. Ulrike. The Audi at Pageant House. Got it. Now, you said you wanted a skirt."

Penny knew that for Frida's skirt to be long enough, it should fall from her own waist to her ankles, so it was easy work to peer at the bottom of the skirt racks and find the longer ones, then try them against her body.

Penny saw one that seemed to fit the bill. "Something like this." She swished the long blue skirt around her legs.

"Nice," said Monica. "I might have a tip for you though. Follow me."

She led the way back outside and showed Izzy a box on the pavement beneath the window. It was labelled SCARECROW CLOTHES, 50P A PIECE.

"See this? Garments that were going to be sent for rags. I had the idea of putting them out for scarecrows, nice and cheap. Why don't you see if there's something in here?"

"Oh I see! It would be better than using nice things, I guess."

Monica shrugged. "When everyone's done with scarecrows these will just end up in the rag bag again."

Penny rootled through until she found a skirt. "Do you know what? This will do nicely. The hem is a bit damaged, but I don't think our scarecrow will mind."

Penny paid Monica and hurried back to Cozy Craft.

"How did you do that?" said Izzy.

"Do what?" said Penny.

"You went out for ice cream and came back with a skirt."

"I've been busy."

"I know," said Izzy. "I've been phoning and you've not picked up."

"Really?" Penny reached for her phone.

"I had news," said Izzy.

There was a throat-clearing cough behind Penny. She whirled and saw Aubrey standing in the shop, a wry smile on his face.

Penny dropped everything and wrapped her arms around his broad chest in a fierce hug. "When did they let you go?"

"Very early this morning," he said. "Denise was worried sick of course, but I thought I'd come back and let you know..." He laughed. "Are you going to hug me all day?"

"Maybe," said Penny. "I'm sorry."

"You're sorry? What for?"

She prised herself away from him, realising there were tears of relief in her eyes. "I— We always seem to get you caught up in some sort of trouble."

"Hijinks," said Izzy helpfully.

"I had noticed," he said.

29

Izzy tried to follow Penny's explanation while they assembled the scarecrow.

"So, this Becky woman had been watching Eve Bennefer's house?"

"Every day," said Penny.

"Then the day after the death at the castle, the jacket is found by Monica outside the charity shop?"

"Bagged up with other charity things, yes."

"And you think this is significant?"

Penny sighed. "Two women are dead. We don't know either of them, but both have claims to being Eve Bennefer. They're linked. And then there's this suspicious woman, Becky, who dumps a distinctive jacket the day after one death and point-blank denies all knowledge of it when I asked her last night."

"Which means what?"

"I don't know. I really don't."

"I'll tell you one thing I know," said Izzy.

"Yes?"

Izzy pointed at the clock on the wall. It was half past three in the afternoon. "We are out of time."

"We really should get on with this scarecrow then?"

"You think?" said Izzy sarcastically, then softened it by grinning.

Penny looked at their construction. "How wide are the arms meant to be?" she asked. "We'll need two broom stales, but do we need to cut one of them down?"

"Maybe it's an urban myth, but aren't we about the same distance, fingertip to fingertip with our arms outstretched, as we are tall?"

"No. Surely not? Let's try."

They got a tape measure and took it in turns to measure each other.

"Well, I never," said Penny. "It *is* true. I guess Frida will be one broom stale tall and one broom stale across."

They made a body from bin bags stuffed with straw, and duct-taped it into place.

"How on earth are we going to get the huipil on her now? It's like she is the worst shape possible to dress up," said Penny.

"Hold on, we can do this." Izzy slid the arms sideways, so Frida suddenly had a really long left arm and a small stump of a right one. "Pop it on the side, then we can go the other way."

The skirt was less of a problem, and finally they put the head on top.

"Gorgeous huipil," said Izzy. "She looks amazing."

"She will look a lot better with a head. Where has that gone?"

"I put it under the counter in case Carmella came in and thought we were making effigies," said Izzy.

Penny laughed at the idea as they put the head on top.

"One day, when we're bored, maybe we should—"

"—No!" Penny said.

"What? How do you know what I was going to say?"

"You were going to suggest we should make a model of Carmella for our own wicked entertainment."

"Yeah, maybe. It would be wrong, though. Very wrong."

"So wrong."

It was gone shop closing time when they were fully done.

"We missed the deadline," said Penny.

"Good job Aubrey gave us a key to the castle gate."

"So we just sneak it in there, plonk it wherever we fancy, and hope no one realises we've made a late addition to the scarecrow walk?"

"Exactly," said Izzy.

They roughly handled their scarecrow creation out of the shop door. Izzy saw Monty crouching low in his basket, eyeing their creation with apprehension.

"I think Monty will be happy to see Frida go – he can't quite decide what she is," she said, gathering the scarecrow's skirts under her arm. "You take the head, I will lead the way with her feet."

They walked the short distance to the castle. Izzy hoped they wouldn't meet any suspicious passers-by, and in that they were lucky. She looked at Pageant House on their way up to the castle and tried not to think of dead bodies and ghosts and curses.

They crossed the bridge, and Izzy unlocked the gate with Aubrey's key.

"There's no burglar alarm to deactivate then?" said Penny.

"I don't think castles needed burglar alarms."

"They've never had us break in before."

They look around the broad green at the heart of the castle, silent and empty of live humans. Dozens of scarecrows were arrayed around the edges of the compound, in a long thin rectangle. Marquee tents and refreshment stands were already erected.

"I'm glad it's not dark," said Izzy. "It would be quite creepy in here with all of those faces looking at you. It's like a haunted house made of mangelwurzel heads."

"This'd be a good place for Frida," said Penny.

The spot, not far from the castle gate, was in the shadow of Stuart Dinktrout's inflated pig blimp balloon. Even thirty feet above their heads, it was a massive wobbling shape: playful pink in colour, with beautiful art nouveau lettering on its side.

"Who goes out and commissions a huge pig balloon?" said Penny.

"I've met Arabella up close and personal," said Izzy. "I can say the real one isn't as rotund as that."

"Yes, well, the real Arabella hasn't been pumped full of fizzy lifting gas."

"Helium."

"That's the one. Ah, look: the scarecrows are all wired into place."

"There's a wire around the fence they are all fastened to," said Izzy, testing it with her fingertips. "My mum does this with her sweet peas. It's like someone's a keen gardener."

"To be fair, the scarecrows need to be secure when this is open to the public. They are not the most stable things in the world."

They pushed the bottom of their scarecrow into the sandy trench and fastened its arms to the wire. They stood back to admire their work.

"Looks good! I do think we have a nice spot here," said Penny. She glanced at the gate, then looked at Izzy. "While we're here…"

"Yes?" said Izzy, slowly.

"That thing Aubrey said the other day – about where the woman fell from. He suggested she had fallen from a window on the level below, and not the castle wall at all. That would explain why no one saw her or the person she was with go past."

"You want to go check?"

Penny gave her a playful look. "We *are* here. There's no one around to stop us. Come on…"

They hurried to the foot of the stairs by the wall and climbed rapidly. The castle walls were high, and Izzy felt that strange exhilaration of simply being at an elevated height: the new perspective; the sense of being literally and figuratively above it all.

"Oh, it's nice up here," she said. "Feel that breeze."

Penny was pacing out along the stone battlements.

"Aubrey was here," she said, pointing at the jolly bunting flags along the inner wall. "Monica was over there. Which means—" she hurried along to the tower halfway between the two positions. "—the woman – I still think of her as Eve Bennefer – was here."

Izzy looked over the wall. It was a dizzying drop to the ground below. For a construction that was over seven hundred years old, the castle was an impressive feat of massive engineering. "That's a terrifying drop."

"She screamed," said Penny. "As she fell, she screamed. I can still hear her."

Izzy put her hand on Penny's shoulder. Penny looked out across the land. The evening sun cast a mass of shadow and red reflections across the mere.

"Remi would have been out there," said Penny. "Taking his photos."

"Two people on the battlements," said Izzy. "Like us."

Penny pointed down. "There is a window down there – on the level below."

"High enough to kill you if you fell from it?" said Izzy.

"I don't know."

"Let's go see."

30

Penny and Izzy made their way back to the castle stairs and descended a level to a dark inner corridor. Izzy used her phone as a torch to light their way along the corridor. "Here," she said. "It would be this window."

The window in question wasn't exactly an arrow slit, but it was very narrow and high up in a sloping recess. Penny thought it might have been what was called an embrasure.

"You think she could have got through there?" she said.

"I don't know. Maybe. Why don't you try?"

"Fling myself out of the same window that Eve fell out of?"

"I was thinking more about trying to fit through without doing any actual flinging. Go on."

Penny huffed as though she didn't think she should be the one doing the climbing and squeezing. She pushed herself up the embrasure's bottom slope, grabbed the sill of the narrow window, and pulled herself towards it. Izzy grabbed the soles of her feet and gave a helpful push.

"Be sure you're not going to fling me out," Penny grunted.

"That would be a terrible thing and I will avoid it if at all possible."

"If at all possible..." Penny muttered. She'd got herself as far as the window. She opened it and pushed her head through. "I don't think I can squeeze through. I'd have to rotate my shoulder and *nnh*— No. Can't do it."

"Okay."

"Also..." Penny slid back down and onto the corridor floor. "Also, I just don't think it's high enough."

"People can break their necks falling off stepladders," said Izzy.

"But I heard her scream it. It was a long scream."

"How long?"

Penny finished brushing dust off her clothes. "I don't know." She looked up thoughtfully, took a deep breath, and produced a subdued falsetto scream for a couple of seconds.

"That long?"

"Yes. I think so."

"Can you do it again?"

"Are you just trying to make me look a fool?"

"I've already done that many times. No. There's a method to my madness." Izzy opened the stopwatch on her phone. "Go."

Penny gave a proper scream this time. Izzy paused the stopwatch. "Two and a half seconds. Just over."

"Is anybody there?" came a distant voice.

Izzy clutched onto Penny. "You hear that?"

"I heard that."

"It's Black Boots the ghost!"

"Or just someone wondering who's screaming."

"We should be alone here."

"We should."

Together, crouched low and pressed close together, they crept along the corridor to the stairs. They peered down into the castle grounds. A woman stood inside the castle gate, her hand moving as though locking the door.

"Carmella! What is she doing here?" Penny hissed.

For a woman who normally swept through life as if she was a cut above everyone else, Carmella Mountjoy was moving in a manner that could only be described as furtive. She was inspecting the scarecrows one by one.

Izzy led the way downstairs. The gloom of evening was deepening and she reasoned that if they could keep quiet, Carmella might not notice them at all.

Carmella was busy unfastening a scarecrow from the wire fencing which linked them all. As they reached the end of the scarecrow line, Izzy pulled Penny closer.

"Pretend to be a scarecrow." Izzy grabbed a hat off a nearby scarecrow and jammed it on her head, then she stuck out her arms and backed into the line of dummies.

Penny started to make small noises of protest, before curiosity got the better of her and she followed suit.

Izzy looked out of the corner of her eyes at Carmella. She carried the uprooted scarecrow to the end of the line near the castle gate. Penny and Izzy stayed as still as they could, but they needn't have worried: Carmella's focus was very much on finding a different spot for the scarecrow.

"That'll be her own scarecrow," said Penny out of the corner of her mouth.

"Looking for a better spot," Izzy agreed. "Such a diva."

Carmella held up her scarecrow, measuring available spaces and made a "Hmm" noise, deciding whether it was the right space or not.

Eventually she put her scarecrow down on the floor, deciding upon some other course of action. She went over to Frida Kahlo and started to loosen the fastenings on the arms.

Izzy couldn't take any more. She stepped forward and shouted. "What on earth are you doing, Carmella?"

31

It was an undoubtedly delicious moment, seeing the shock and surprise play out across Carmella's face. She had been caught in the act of doing something underhand. Naturally, being Carmella, she attempted to brazen it out.

"How irresponsible to hide in the shadows and scare people!" she retorted. "You two are as dreadful as ever!"

"Dreadful? Us?"

"As it happens, I am doing a little rearranging. I was asked to do this because of my well-honed instinct for a good display."

"Really? The festival organisers approved this?"

"My Frank is a trustee of the castle."

Penny made a show of looking round. "I don't see him anywhere. And I know Stuart Dinktrout's views on giving you the best spot. It looks very much as though you are trying to put your own creation in a more advantageous position, while removing ours from its prime spot."

Penny leaned over to whisper in Izzy's ear. "Keep her talking, I will go round the back and secure Frida from the other side."

"Good plan," Izzy whispered back.

Carmella advanced on Izzy as Penny slipped round to the side. "So you admit that you are here to take the best position?"

"Take?"

"What gives you the right to complain about me doing the exact same thing?"

"We just brought our scarecrow and put it in a spare spot," said Izzy. "In fact, if I had to guess, I would suggest this space was set aside for our creation, because it was blindingly obvious it was the best of the lot."

Izzy was not naturally a combative person, but there was something in Carmella's superior manner that brought out the worst in her. Izzy held Carmella's incredulous and disdainful glare before going in for the kill.

"Let's see what yours is, shall we?" Izzy strode forward and looked at the scarecrow which Carmella had brought in. She stared down at the green face. "Is this a witch?"

"Not just any witch," said Carmella. "It's Elphaba, from *Wicked*. She is wearing some of the original costuming from the first West End production! I know people, you see. This is a very special creation."

"And there was me thinking it was just your spare witch costume."

"Oh! So rude!"

"Seriously, Carmella, she could be your twin."

Carmella roared with rage and jabbed a finger at Izzy. "You two are the worst kind of people. Not only do you continue to sully my business with your feeble attempts to compete and steal my customers, but you do it with the utter crassness of ... of—"

"—of youth, perhaps?"

Carmella was right in Izzy's face now, snarling as if she meant to bite.

"Mm, garlic," said Izzy, wafting a hand in front of her face "You must teach me your sophisticated ways, Carmella."

"Sorted!" called Penny from the other side of the fence.

"Sorted? What's sorted?" asked Carmella, stepping back as if she only just remembered what she was actually doing.

"Now why don't you find a space for your scarecrow somewhere else," said Izzy. "Then we can lock up and all go home."

"I don't think so!" roared Carmella. "Seriously, don't you think my husband will have something to say to Stuart if my scarecrow is to be put in the cheap seats? I will not tolerate this sort of behaviour."

She went over to Frida Kahlo and started tugging fiercely at it. "What is this anyway? Some sort of Carmen Miranda with bad eyebrows?"

"It's fine," Penny said to Izzy. "I found the end of some rope, so Frida is very much fastened to the wire there. Carmella will never get it loose without breaking her and tearing the fence down."

"Nice work," said Izzy.

They stood for a moment, watching Carmella grunting and heaving at their scarecrow.

"Come on," said Penny. "Give it up, Carmella. This is undignified."

"You don't think I can do this, do you?" Carmella huffed. "Well let me tell you that I am a Yogalates black belt. I am much stronger than you imagine!"

"Can you be a black belt in Yogalates?" asked Penny.

"What even is Yogalates?" asked Izzy.

Carmella had hold of Frida around the middle,. She braced her legs against the fence to get more purchase. "It will come off, I guarantee it!" she screamed through gritted teeth.

"One thing I didn't check," said Penny thoughtfully. "How the wire itself is secured."

At that moment there was a popping sound as something came loose. Carmella fell backwards to the ground. Frida the scarecrow had finally come away from the fence, dragging wire and the rope with it.

"You're just damaging things now," said Penny.

Izzy stared at the taut rope. It seemed to be tugging at an unusual angle. More vertical than she might have imagined. "Where did you get the spare rope from anyway?" she asked, looking about in the diminishing light.

Penny shrugged. "It was an end piece, threaded through a hoop in the ground. I don't think it was joined to anything."

Izzy pointed. "I think maybe it was."

Stuart Dinktrout's big pig balloon wobbled in the air and rose.

Carmella fell back as Frida Kahlo was pulled skywards by the balloon.

"What have you done, Carmella?" gasped Penny.

"I think it might have been a joint effort," said Izzy. "Was the rope in the hoop on a quick release knot by any chance?"

"I don't know."

"Like a mooring hitch or a buntline hitch?"

"I don't know knots!" Penny shouted.

Quick!" Izzy yelled. "Grab hold of Frida!"

The three of them launched themselves at the hovering scarecrow.

"We need to get that thing tied back down!" Izzy shouted. She pulled at the upright broom stale, but it came loose without any significant resistance and clattered to the ground. She grabbed Frida's skirts, and tried to pull the scarecrow down. Carmella and Penny did the same, hauling on the arms.

There was a gust of wind and they were all swept off their feet. Izzy fell away, while Penny and Carmella still held on.

Izzy watched as they rose, rapidly. They were three feet above the ground, then six.

"Let go! Let go! While you can!"

They both let go and fell to the earth.

"Is everyone all right?" Izzy said, concerned, but no one seemed to be paying attention. They watched as the rising balloon took the wire backing with it and, with almost no resistance, plucked the next scarecrow out of the ground.

"Oh, heck!" Penny whispered. "They're all tied together."

Carmella waved her arms at the spectacle unfolding. "It's

taking all of the others with it! Look! Bob the Builder and ... and what's the fish from *Hunting Nimmo*?"

"*Finding Nemo!*" Penny hissed.

"Whatever!"

Carmella was right. The wire supporting the scarecrows was securely joined to the rising balloon. It popped free of the fence with audible pinging sounds every few seconds. More scarecrows joined Frida Kahlo, floating into the sky. "It's one of the Beatles, look!" shouted Izzy.

"That is Mick Jagger," said Carmella with disdain. "Don't they teach you anything in school?"

"Hopefully, there will come a point where the combined weight is too much and it stops the balloon," said Izzy. Even as she said it, she knew she was kidding herself. As the balloon rose higher, above the height of the castle wall, it caught the refreshing breeze and was swept sideways at great speed. The three of them had to sprint away to avoid getting caught up by a wire that now lashed like a snake's tail. The scarecrows were coming away at speed now, a chain of celebrity straw figures.

"Ed Sheeran, no!" yelled Penny. Then she crumpled and wailed in despair. "And Fred and Ginger! Oh, poor Nanna Lem!"

"Wait, where's dad's Elvis one?" yelled Izzy. "I can't let him lose his Elvis costume." She ran along and found it towards the end. "No, Elvis! Don't leave me now!"

She launched herself at the scarecrow, grunting hard with an irrational idea that she could make herself heavier through an act of sheer will. She was whipped into the air with the last of the line, clinging onto the cape she and

Penny had spent so long embellishing. "*Noo*—!" She swung in the air, briefly toying with the idea of sticking with Elvis until the whole thing came to earth somewhere. Then she fell away, knowing it was way too risky and ultimately useless.

Ping! Ping! Ping!

The final fastenings snapped loose. All of the scarecrows were airborne, trailing after the balloon like the strings of an enormous kite.

The three of them watched it rise and rise, floating away out of reach.

"Elvis has left the building, said Penny numbly.

32

"Well," said Carmella, licking her dry lips nervously. "That's torn it. All your fault, of course."

Izzy knew Carmella was blustering. The steam had gone out of her attack. She knew who was very much in the firing line when it came to the blame.

"We have jointly caused this situation," said Penny carefully.

"I'm taking no blame for this," said Carmella automatically. "You should have held onto them, stopped them floating away."

"You're taking all the blame," said Izzy immediately. "I didn't see you holding onto them."

"I have a terrible fear of heights. It's a medical affliction," said Carmella. "Anything more than a dozen feet off the ground and I become quite bilious."

The balloon and its unusual cargo were swaying silhouettes in the sky.

"Jointly to blame," said Penny. "So, we need to jointly solve it."

"I'm open to suggestions," said Carmella.

"Maybe if we just own up and tell Stuart immediately, he can get the police to track the thing with their, um, their…"

Izzy gave Penny a hug. "I'm not sure what the end of that sentence might have been, but whatever equipment is needed to track rogue balloons trailing scarecrows, I don't think the police have it. Also, it would take about a week for Stuart to stop shouting and ask them for it."

"It's very simple," said Carmella.

"Yes?" said Penny.

"We start a fire."

Penny and Izzy looked at her.

"You might need to expand on that statement," said Izzy.

"A nice cleansing fire to sweep away the evidence. Make it look as though everything went up in flames," said Carmella. "An accident."

Izzy's eyebrows shot up. "Whoa – hang on now! Penny: I can see you are drawn to the idea of doing the honourable thing, but I think we can all see some immediate problems with that. Carmella: I can understand the attraction of a nice cleansing fire, but it's highly likely to create a much bigger problem."

"Like what?" Carmella snarled.

"You want to set fire to a castle."

"Castles don't burn. They're just stone."

"Tell that to Windsor Castle. Nobody is setting anything

on fire. Let's just establish that right now as a ground rule, shall we?"

"No fires," Penny agreed. "Now, let's work on some other solutions, shall we? Who has any other ideas?"

They all looked at each other.

"Well, I think I might head off and sleep on it," said Carmella with a huge artificial yawn. "I'm sure something will occur to me in the morning." She made to leave, but Izzy grabbed her arm.

"Carmella Mountjoy, do I have to spell this out? I know what's in your head. You're going off to blab to Stuart, or Frank, or maybe both of them. You will try and drop Penny and me into trouble. But guess what? If you do that we will double down and make sure *everyone* knows who pulled that scarecrow off the fence, after breaking in here after hours to do mischief."

Carmella looked as if she wanted to say something, then sagged in defeat.

"None of us can leave here until we have an answer. Like it or not, we need to sort this out between the three of us." Izzy stared hard until Carmella gave a small, reluctant nod.

"So can we blame someone else?" Carmella asked. "We could say we saw some rough types breaking in here."

"Rough types," repeated Penny, slightly incredulous.

"You know," said Carmella. "Outsiders. Travellers. Ne'er-do-wells."

"Okay. Someone read too many Enid Blyton *Famous Five* books as a girl," said Penny. "Rough types? Blooming heck, Carmella. No."

Izzy shook her head. "If we start a huge manhunt, we could make things worse. Imagine if we were found out?"

Carmella shrugged lightly.

"What if we re-made the scarecrows?" Penny said.

"Re-made them? There were at least twenty!" said Carmella, scoffing. "We wouldn't have a hope."

"Wait, let's think it through before we dismiss it," said Izzy. "If we managed to keep everyone out of here, how much time would we have?"

Carmella rolled her eyes. "The judging isn't until Sunday – but seriously? We can't do all of that tomorrow!"

"It's not tomorrow yet," said Izzy. "It's still Friday evening for a bit. We'd have the rest of tonight, all of Saturday, and Sunday morning. Maybe thirty-six hours. That's more than an hour per scarecrow.

"So we just, what, go without sleep?" Carmella looked horrified. "I really don't function well without a solid eight hours."

Izzy paced as she processed her thoughts, ignoring Carmella. "I can see quite a few difficulties we would need to overcome, but it is the only idea that comes close to being achievable."

"But—" Carmella started.

Izzy held up a hand. "There's a lot to do. We need to get serious with planning. Much as it pains me to say it, we need to start making a list of potential problems and then brainstorm ways to solve them. Let's secure the castle gate and go round to the shop."

They all trouped out, and Penny secured the lock.

"Won't Stuart notice his massive balloon has gone?" said

Izzy. "I guess that is one of the things we need to brainstorm. We'll add that to the list of things to do."

There was a tiny exclamation of "Yay, lists!" from Penny.

"I'm starting to think the whole castle is cursed," said Izzy.

"Cursed?" said Carmella.

"Oh, don't," said Penny. "There are no dark magic curses."

"I didn't say it was dark magic," said Izzy. "It could be just ... bad energy."

"Bad energy," Penny scoffed.

"Oh, bad energy is a thing," said Carmella seriously. "What we do sends out karmic ripples into the world."

Izzy nodded in agreement. Penny looked like she wanted to argue but didn't have the energy.

"There are tales of ghosts and such attached to the castle," said Izzy. "That woman fell from the walls not four days ago. Then that other woman died in Pageant House."

"Not in the castle grounds," said Penny.

"The whole area could have bad juju," said Carmella, moving her hands in a circular motion.

"And now this has happened to us," said Izzy.

"Bad energy, bad luck," Carmella concurred.

Penny sighed. "Anything can be made to look bad if you only pick bad examples. Er – for example, it was just down there that Monty found that bag of cash. That's good luck."

"Not for the person who lost it," Izzy pointed out.

"Huh," said Carmella. "I thought you just made that story up to get your faces in the local press."

33

Penny put on all the lights in the shop. Monty sat up in his basket and made a querying noise at the sight of Carmella Mountjoy before settling down to continue his snooze.

Izzy sorted out an enormous piece of pattern drafting paper and smoothed it onto the wall, squeezing blu-tack behind the corners.

"I'll start," said Carmella, grabbing a pen. "My organisational skills are legendary."

"We're not organising yet, we are brainstorming," said Penny, gently prising the pen from Carmella's fingers. "We can use your skills once we know everything we need to do."

"And I suppose you are an expert at brainstorming?" said Carmella.

"I am merely the facilitator," said Penny. "We all need to bring our very best brainstorming, and I will capture it. Now, what are the areas we need to consider?"

"Obviously, re-building scarecrows," said Izzy.

Penny circled it in the centre of the paper, and then paused with the pen. "So, do we know what they all were? The scarecrows, I mean."

There was a pause.

"Fine, I will capture it for now. 'Get list of scarecrows'," said Penny, writing it as another bubble.

"Sourcing supplies," shouted Izzy. "Seriously, I think we sold all of the mangelwurzels and the broom stales."

"Hm, yes." Penny wrote it down with a shake of her head.

"And, can I state the very obvious fact that even if we knew what a scarecrow was supposed to be, the idea that we can make it look like the original entry is laughable!" said Carmella.

"Again with the negative attitude, Carmella!" said Penny, wagging the pen at her. "Can we rephrase, so it sounds more like a task or a problem we can solve?"

"Fine. Let's call it 'Get visual references for scarecrows'." Carmella shook her head as if she was surrounded by idiots.

"There's the balloon-related tasks," said Izzy. "Like, making sure that Stuart doesn't notice it's missing. Also, finding the balloon."

"Yes, distracting Stuart will be key," said Penny, writing it down.

"Hang on," said Izzy, "I think you're solutionising."

Penny paused and looked back at her. "How do you mean? It's what we just said, isn't it? We need to make sure Stuart doesn't see his balloon is missing. We need to distract him."

"Orrrrrr..." Izzy walked around in a circle, looking up at

the ceiling as she stretched the word out to last as long as she could.

"Is your sister having a medical episode?" whispered Carmella to Penny.

"She is my *cousin*, and she is having an idea," said Penny. She frowned. "I think."

"Orrrrr, we make it look as though the balloon is still there. Imagine if we put a *little* balloon up there and made it look *massive* to Stuart, by changing the prescription on his glasses or something."

There was a stunned silence.

"Erm, I know we are at the brainstorming part, and we are not supposed to criticise ideas, but that seems ... unlikely to work," said Penny.

"Fine. I just wanted to make a point," said Izzy. "We state the need and *then* come up with solutions."

"Good, that's clear. We can move on and do that now I think. First of all, who has ideas on how we can get the list of entries?" Penny asked.

"We can list all the ones we can remember, for a start," said Carmella.

"Stuart must have a list," said Izzy. "I can pretend we'll need it for the Frambeat Gazette. I mean, we *will* need it, but I can email him and ask for it now."

"Sounds like we can start from what we remember, then hopefully address the blanks when we get the full list," said Penny, adding detail to the board. "Now then, getting any kind of visual reference would be an absolute godsend. Where might we find visual references for the scarecrows?"

"Social media?" said Carmella.

Penny was mildly impressed that Carmella was joining in with problem solving. "Yep. Good shout."

"Tariq could be our best bet," said Izzy. "If he started taking pics, he will have loads. I will text him."

Carmella pulled a face. "Look, even if we managed to get good pictures of every single one, which I doubt we will, what are the chances we can accurately recreate them all? It just seems a bit ... impossible."

Penny took a deep breath. "Carmella, are we a group of people who would normally choose to spend time together? No. But if I had to choose a team to pull off something impossible, would it be this group here? Again, no. But I think we *could* be that group. There are a diverse set of perspectives in this room – that's something we cannot deny. We also have creative talent coming out of our ears. Let's set aside all negative thoughts and go for it. We haven't come up with any solid alternatives, so we need to give it a go. If the scarecrows look a bit different once we're done then we can brazen it out, I reckon."

"Brazen, yes," said Carmella.

It was a veiled insult, but also a concession. Carmella wasn't naturally a team player, but she was still in the room.

"There is a trade-off to be made, in that case," said Carmella. "In terms of quality. I think we are effectively saying we will compromise on quality in order to do this in time."

"Yes, I think we are definitely saying that," said Izzy.

"So that will inform this other item you have up here on the board," said Carmella, striding forward and tapping the paper with a polished fingernail. "Sourcing supplies. If we're compromising on quality, then we should try to source supplies that will make this quick and easy."

"What does that mean, exactly?" asked Penny. "We haven't got time to order a dozen head-shaped things off the internet."

"What time does the Co-op shut? One of us should go over there quickly and buy everything that is round off the fruit and veg aisle. If it's bigger than a grapefruit then we can use it," said Carmella.

"I'll go!" shouted Izzy. She grabbed a bag and ran.

The door had barely closed when Penny's phone buzzed with a message. She read it and sighed.

"Problems?" said Carmella.

"I was supposed to go on a date tonight. He's just texting me to ask where I'd like to go." Miserably, Penny began to compose a text to Remi telling him she was no longer available. "Maybe the castle *is* cursed," she muttered.

34

The Co-op supermarket was the largest shop in Framlingham and stayed open until ten at night most days. Izzy picked up a wire basket as she burst through its doors. She thought for a moment, then swapped it for a trolley to better manage the weight. Hopefully there would be lots of head-shaped things available.

She headed straight to the section for root vegetables, but of course there were no mangelwurzels. She wanted to ask if they had any, but that was only so she could say it out loud, and there was no time for such indulgence. They had turnips, but they were all a bit small. Izzy weighed one in her hand, then fetched a grapefruit for reference. She tried it against a few turnips, and found there was only one that was large enough. She put it into the trolley, along with the swedes, which looked like sad, shrunken mangelwurzels, but she was in no position to be fussy.

What else was there?

"Melons," she declared to herself.

Izzy found there were only four melons. As she put them in the trolley, something else caught her eye. It was a display featuring local vegetables, and made much of their Suffolk heritage. It featured some really huge onions. She had never seen onions of that size. They were definitely bigger than grapefruit, so into the trolley they went, all five of them. She trundled round the rest of the shop, hoping for some footballs, but there were none. She did find some tights, so she put a few packets in with her haul and wheeled the trolley over to pay.

"Doing some cooking?" asked the assistant with a smile.

"Yes, it's a Polish recipe," said Izzy automatically, before hurrying off with her bags bulging.

Izzy was back inside with Penny and Carmella in a few moments and she put the bags on the floor. "We can unpack later." She pulled out her phone as she got her breath back.

"While you were out, Carmella and I jotted down the scarecrows we could remember seeing," said Penny. "We're up to fourteen."

"Well, after checking my messages I have some good news and some bad news," said Izzy.

"Don't play games," growled Carmella. "Just tell us."

"Fine. Well, the good news is that Stuart has sent me the full list of entries. The bad news is that Tariq has no photos so far. He's blaming a tummy bug, says he was going to catch up over the weekend."

"Oh no, that's another person who we need to keep

away," said Carmella with a dramatic groan. "I need a drink. Do you have anything in here?"

"I'll put the kettle on," said Penny.

"Not tea! I meant wine," said Carmella.

"Tea might be a better idea," said Penny. "So we can be at our best later on."

Carmella huffed and rolled her eyes. "Fine. Let's look at this list from Stuart, shall we? We can at least fill in the gaps on ours."

Izzy showed Carmella the list. "There are seventeen on here, so there should only be three missing. You and Penny did well."

They ran through Stuart's list, with Carmella writing down the ones that were missing.

"This can't be right. We're up to twenty now."

Penny came downstairs with a tray of tea and biscuits. "What's wrong?"

"Stuart's list and our list are not matching very well. We probably need to see if we have written down something that we've misinterpreted, as Stuart should have taken his list from the entry forms. If we can't explain it that way, then there are some extra entries that Stuart doesn't have on his list."

"Ooh yes, best to get them off the list at this point."

They all glanced back and forth between the two lists.

"Oh, I bet Captain Jack Sparrow should really have been Keith Richards," said Carmella. "Understandable mistake." She crossed out the entry on her list.

"Here's another one, we had 'Teen Wolf" – you know, the

one with a canine head and the yellow jacket. I suppose that's meant to be 'Freddie Mongrelly'," said Penny.

"Freddie Mongrelly?" said Carmella.

"A pun. It's that classic fist in the air Freddie Mercury pose but it's a dog. Freddie Mongrelly."

It took them several long minutes before Carmella spoke again. "Do you think it's possible the one we had as Cher was actually King Charles II? It had poodle hair and a velvet top. I can picture it now."

Izzy and Penny looked at each other and shrugged.

"If that is the case, then I think we now have an accurate list," declared Carmella, making the corrections with a flourish.

Izzy led them in a polite round of applause for themselves.

"We are making good progress," said Penny. "But we haven't yet tackled the question about how we manage Stuart, and stop him noticing we have destroyed everything. Who has ideas?"

"I imagine you will poo-poo anything that involves hospitalising him?" Carmella said lightly.

Izzy could see Penny searching for the right words. "Shall we try and focus on ideas that don't involve harming people?" she tried. "There must be a way of keeping him occupied. Could you persuade your husband to do something, Carmella?"

"Frank? Are you mad? He and Stuart can't stand each other!"

"But they are very competitive. Could Frank pretend there is a pig competition on or something?"

Carmella chewed a lip in thought. "Maybe there is something in what you say."

"Ooh, ooh! I know!" said Izzy, jigging with excitement. "We put a note from Frank through Stuart's door and a note from Stuart through Frank's door, both challenging the other to a pig race somewhere quite far away!"

"A pig race?" said Penny.

"A pig race," said Izzy.

"Hah!" Carmella's laugh was rich and fruity, a proper belly laugh. "That would simply be too funny! The only bad thing would be that we couldn't be there to watch them."

"Is it the kind of thing they would both fall for?" said Penny.

"Oh, my negative Nelly, it's a bizarre and unexpected bet, the kind of outlandish wager that Victorian gentlemen might make. If I word it correctly, neither of them would be able to resist. I shall send them both to a beach at the behest of an invented individual. Which beach? Somewhere far enough away to keep them from here, but not so far as to put them off."

"Great Yarmouth," said Penny.

Carmella frowned. "If we must. It's a bit tacky and tawdry for my tastes."

"I'm sorry, I've just got Great Yarmouth on the brain for some reason."

"What a terrible affliction. Right, I will see to that. Leave it with me." Carmella pulled the pad of paper towards her and sat in thought for a moment, composing her invitation to the fake pig racing event. "Hm," she said. "Ideally they should end up actually having a race, to make sure it keeps them busy." She jotted some notes. "Oh, weren't we also going to figure out how to stop Tariq from snooping round and exposing us?"

"Here's the thing," said Izzy. "I think we might need to bring Tariq in and tell him what's going on."

Carmella spluttered angrily. "Why on earth would you do that?"

"Well, for one, because he is really nosey. If anyone is going to figure out something is wrong, it's him. But also because we can use his help in tracking the balloon. He has a drone, so he might be able to find it from the sky."

"That balloon might be miles away by now," said Carmella. "But fine, send him off on a wild goose chase in his car and see if he can find it." She looked at Penny and Izzy as they exchanged a glance. "What? He does have a car, doesn't he?"

35

Penny opened the door of the shop and let Tariq Jazeel and Remi De Smet inside. It was now fully dark outside and both of them looked mildly concerned at the situation. "Please come in," said Penny. "We'll get you a cup of tea and explain everything."

They stepped into the shop, which Penny realised had now been turned into something like a war room combined with a nascent production line. Izzy barged in through the door behind them, dragging a pair of bulging bin liners.

"I hit pay dirt! The rag bin at the back of the charity shop was full of discarded clothing, so I brought it all over," she yelled over her shoulder. "*And* I found a pile of discarded wood from a fence that's being replaced. Well I hope it was discarded. Oh – hello." Izzy straightened and smoothed her clothing once she realised they had visitors.

"I was about to explain the situation to Tariq and Remi," said Penny.

"Hold up Penny," said Tariq, in a theatrical whisper. "I don't know if you know this, but Carmella Mountjoy is sitting over there."

Penny saw Carmella roll her eyes, having definitely heard the comment.

"Yes Tariq," said Penny. "This situation involves Carmella. We are working together."

"But you hate her! She is your enemy!" Tariq hissed.

"I can hear you, you know," said Carmella. "And for the record, I am not here because I wish to be."

"Today we are setting aside our differences, because we find ourselves in a bit of a pickle," said Penny. "Jointly. It's a joint pickle." She went on to explain to the two men what had happened with the scarecrows and the pig-shaped balloon.

Remi nodded and raised his eyebrows many times, but remained silent.

Tariq looked as if he was about to explode with questions. "You mean to tell me that the pig balloon took off into the sky with all those scarecrows hanging on a string?" His eyes were saucer-wide as his hand mimed the action, wafting up, up and away.

"Yes."

"And nobody got a picture? Tragic. That would go *so* viral, I can see it now."

"Now we get to the crux of things, Tariq," said Izzy, coming round and facing him. "It is very important that you understand we do not want pictures of this to be circulated, however tempting it might be. We are attempting to rectify this situation *before* everyone finds out."

"Fine. No pictures." Tariq's face suggested he wasn't convinced. Penny thought they might need to reinforce the message later.

"So here's what we were hoping the two of you might help with," said Penny. She beckoned them over to the counter where there was some space, and smoothed out the Ordnance Survey map for the area. "So here's the castle," she said, jabbing a finger at the map. "The balloon went up at around eighteen hundred hours, and I believe it initially moved in a westerly direction." She placed an acrylic ruler across the map.

"Why are you talking as if you're in a spy film?" asked Carmella, coming over to look.

"It's just what you do when you're gathered around a map, doing planning," said Penny. "Now does anyone know how to estimate wind speed?"

"The Beaufort scale maybe?" said Izzy.

Remi nodded knowledgeably. "It is a scale which relates wind speed to observable conditions. Did anyone see any smoking chimneys, flags fluttering, or trees moving?"

There were shrugs all round.

"If we call it a light breeze then it would be between four and seven miles per hour. So, it's now three hours later," said Remi.

Tariq stabbed calculations into his phone.

"Seriously? You need a calculator for that?" Carmella asked. "Somewhere between twelve and twenty one miles to the west. The balloon might be approaching the A14 very soon."

"So we wondered whether you might look for it?" Penny

asked Remi and Tariq. "Remi, you have your motorcycle and sidecar, and Tariq, you have your marvellous new drone."

"Penny, can I just point out that it is nighttime?" said Remi. "I would love to help, but how can we see where the balloon might be when there is no light?"

"I realise that it won't be possible to find it right now, but at sunrise ... maybe you could head out? Please?"

Remi gave Penny a long look. "This was not the evening out I was expecting," he said.

"I'm sorry."

"No," he smiled. "It is oddly entertaining."

Tariq sighed and went back to the map. "So if the sun rises around six, it will be twelve hours since lift-off, and the balloon will be..." he whipped out his phone again.

"Between forty eight and eighty four miles away!" snapped Carmella. "You need a bigger map, and *you* need to practise your mental arithmetic."

"We can take a look," said Remi with a shrug. "It will be an interesting way to see some more of the countryside."

"I guess I can keep an eye on social media while you drive," said Tariq. "It seems like the sort of thing people might post about if they see it."

"Thank you both! Why don't you go and get some sleep. I'll set up a group chat so that we can keep in touch when you head out," said Penny.

36

Izzy opened one of the bin bags she'd brought in.

Carmella stood up and announced she was going to deliver the notes she'd written to Stuart and Frank. "I will be gone for about thirty minutes. When I return, I shall work on some outfits, but I do expect you to have unpacked those disgusting bin bags in my absence. I, for one, will not be sorting through waste."

"Do you think Stuart and Frank will do what you want?" Penny asked.

"They most definitely will. I have hinted that choosing the best side of the beach just after sunrise will be advantageous, so I expect them both to be up and out very early in the morning."

"But won't Frank expect you to join him?" asked Izzy.

"Oh, my dear girl. You have only recently moved in with your man, I believe? Frank and I have been together for a good many years and we both recognise the value of a little space in a marriage. Space gives us the freedom to present our best selves to one another. Frank comes in after a day of loafing about or preening his pigs, and can pretend he is a captain of commerce at the end of a hard day's work. And as he comes in, I strip off my yellow marigolds and pretend I have been wrist deep in soapy washing up, even though all of the work has been done hours before, possibly by a lovely little Greek lady who does for us. I admire him, he admires me, and, in this way, our love grows ever stronger."

With that, Carmella swished out of the shop.

"Do we trust her to come back?" Izzy asked.

"We definitely don't trust her," said Penny, "but she knows she's up to her neck in this now. She can't afford to bail because she thinks we would drop her in it."

"And would we?"

"Most definitely," said Penny. "Now, how shall we divide up the work?"

Izzy made a humming sound. "You know what would be fun? You know when you see American diners on the telly and the short order cooks grab the bits of paper with the orders and cooks them?"

"Tickets. Hotel kitchens use a similar thing," said Penny.

"Well we write all the things we need to make on Post-it notes, we rush forward, grab the ones we plan to make, and make them! Ideally we'd have a bell to hit once we finish one. Ding!"

Penny looked thoughtful. Izzy wondered if she could see the obvious appeal of making it a high-energy game? Maybe she was just thinking about where to find a bell?

"So we would have a ticket that said 'surgeon head', and

another that said 'surgeon body' and we would just grab the ones we planned to work on next?"

"Yes! So maybe it's easiest to do three heads in one go. Who knows? We will figure out efficiencies as we go along."

"Let's do it."

They started writing tickets based on the list, then stuck them up on the planning board. It looked like a lot of tasks, but Izzy was keen to get started.

"You know what strikes me? Some of these heads will be quite intricate, and some will be much easier. Like Sandra Bullock in *Birdbox*. That's the one where she wears a massive blindfold, isn't it? That one will be super easy. I might use an onion for her because it won't matter."

Izzy grabbed the ticket and got to work. She could see Penny eyeing what she was doing as she took a ticket for herself.

"Which one are you going to do?" Izzy called.

"I'm making a body for Dustin from *Stranger Things*, although I'd better unpack those bin bags before her ladyship gets back."

Izzy shrugged. "You'll need some clothes for Dustin, there is bound to be something in there. It's weird how she won't touch those clothes when they are in a rubbish bag, but if we fold them and put them on the side, she will be fine with it. At times like this that I wish I had a toy mouse, or a big rubber spider, so we could pretend there was something horrible in there."

"Honestly, I think Carmella would be more horrified to find supermarket branded clothes."

Izzy held up the enormous onion, and realised that it

formed a better head when placed upside down. Its frizzy roots gave it a distinctive hairstyle. It wasn't helpful for any of their scarecrows, so she formed some hair from a bundle of yarn. Once the blindfold was tied over the face, it just needed a mouth drawn on underneath.

"One head down, seventeen to go!" she yelled.

"Hey, we didn't talk about the boundaries or interfaces between tasks," said Penny.

"Eh? What do you mean?"

"So, when you make a head, are you including a hole for a stick? When I make a body, should I also have a stick?"

"Huh. Well I guess if we don't do that then we would have a whole load of extra work. Fine, I will make a hole." Izzy fetched a knife.

Carmella returned just before midnight. "Here I am, mission accomplished!" she crowed as she came in through the door. She hadn't got halfway across the floor when she wrinkled her nose in disgust. "What is *that smell*?"

"Prize winning local onions," said Izzy, holding up the knife. "Beggars can't be choosers when it comes to available head-shaped things. However, I think we're just discovering the main downside to using onions."

Penny explained the ticket system to Carmella, who walked over to inspect the pieces of paper.

"Fred Astaire and Ginger Rogers sound like bodies I could tackle." She carried the tickets over to the far end of the cutting table and studied them carefully – as if a scribbled ticket might have more details to share. She then walked around the shop, inspecting the rolls of fabric.

Izzy could see Carmella was drawn to a roll of expensive

silk, embellished with sequins. Izzy coughed lightly, and when Penny looked up gave a nod to indicate what Carmella was doing.

Carmella lifted up the roll to carry it over to her workstation.

Penny stepped forward. "While we're all happy to donate resources to this project as needed, I think we need to be mindful of costs. Did you look through the items that we recovered from the charity shop?"

Carmella scowled. "I wasn't aware that my creativity would be constrained in this way. How can I work if I am denied access to what I need?"

"Carmella, no scarecrow needs a silk fabric that costs fifty pounds a metre, especially when I'm certain there is a perfectly lovely evening gown in that pile there, which is free – apart from the donation I will make to Community Change in the morning, so that I am not tormented by the guilt."

Penny took the fabric from Carmella and put it back, then she rifled through the charity shop pile and pulled out a dress.

"Apricot?" said Carmella. "I'm not sure Ginger Rogers would have ever worn that."

"Wasn't she mostly in black and white anyway?" asked Izzy. "I'm sure she won't mind. Not that I've ever really watched any of their films, I don't think."

"Philistine," said Carmella.

"I watched *Top Hat* the other night" Penny said. "Monty and I liked it."

Monty whined in his basket.

"You *did* like it," Penny told him. "Basically, Fred Astaire is this American tap dancer who falls in love with Ginger Rogers while in London. But she mistakes Fred for his friend, Horace, who is also Ginger's friend's husband. So Ginger thinks Fred is a would-be adulterer and a cad. And, as they say, hilarity ensues." She turned to Carmella. "Use the apricot. Look at it as a test of your creativity, yes? I am certain you can rise to the challenge. When it comes to Fred Astaire there won't be a tux and a top hat, but I am convinced you can adapt something from here to suit."

"To suit! I see what you did there!" said Izzy.

"I'm not certain I can work here all night with the sound of you two jabbering," said Carmella, snatching the dress from Penny.

"Fine. Feel free to set the standard," said Izzy. "Start a conversation that is more to your liking."

"Maybe silence is more to my liking?" Carmella huffed. "Very well. Let's talk about sewing, as it's what we all have in common."

"Nice! What's your favourite thing to sew, Carmella?" asked Izzy.

"Hm, good question." Carmella lugged a bin liner filled with straw over to her workstation and started to squeeze it into shape around one of the wooden stakes before she slipped the dress onto it. "I always enjoy the final embellishments. Often it will be the hem or something that needs to be sewn by hand. If I can sit quietly and enjoy holding the near-finished garment, it is always quite joyful."

Izzy reeled slightly, hearing Carmella describe an emotional connection to her work. She had never imagined Carmella having an emotional connection to anything. "That is quite lovely. I tend to like hand sewing less, mainly because it's slow, but I should show it some more appreciation."

"Ah, the youthful need for speed," said Carmella. "I suppose you press the pedal to the metal at every opportunity?"

"Izzy prefers to treadle," said Penny.

"Treadling? No!" Carmella put her hands on her hips. "Why on earth would you do that when we have electricity?"

"Because it's pleasant. The sewing machine goes as fast as I need it to go, and it's nice to think I can make that happen with a gentle flipping of my feet."

"Gentle? It sounds exhausting! Surely you get out of puff?"

"Have you ever seen a treadle in action, Carmella?" asked Izzy.

"No, I don't think so. It's a bit like using a mangle to do the washing. I would rather distance myself from such primitive ideas."

"Well maybe I will show you. It's not like an exercise bike where you have to pedal like a mad thing."

"Here!" called Penny. "I need some fringe stitching onto my Mick Jagger scarf, maybe you could use that to show Carmella."

Izzy opened out the treadle and beckoned Carmella to take a look. "My feet on the treadle and – go!"

It was a few moments' work to apply the fringing.

"Hm, that is a lot less frantic than I had imagined," said Carmella. "Soothing, almost. I would be interested to have a go at some point."

37

"Is it starting to get light outside?" asked Penny. She was tired, but also wired with adrenalin. It was as if the rest of the world's reality was waiting outside, while here in the shop was a strange bubble world. So strange that Carmella Mountjoy was working alongside them re-making scarecrows with a concentrated intensity.

The heads and bodies were piling up, and at least half of the tickets had moved from the board to the edges of the workstations as they completed their tasks.

"We should take a look at the gaps we have in our supplies," said Izzy. "We can see where we are going to need things, and once the rest of the world is awake we can start to get them."

"Did anyone see the *Finding Nemo* scarecrow?" asked Penny, picking up the ticket. "It seems like a really unlikely subject for a scarecrow. I can't even picture it."

"I did see it," said Carmella, thoughtfully. "It was like a regular scarecrow with that Nimmo for its head."

"Nemo. Well that is a relief." Penny heard her phone buzz so went to check it. "Oh, Tariq says that he and Remi are on the road already. They wanted to beat the traffic and get over towards Cambridge for first light."

"Nice! They are on the ball," said Izzy.

"Have they a plan what to do if they find it?" asked Carmella. She looked at both Penny and Izzy, who were silent. "I mean, let's say we get a best-case scenario where they find the whole lot has come down in a field. They can't exactly tuck it into a sidecar and bring it all back, can they?"

"No..." said Penny, thinking hard. "No. I don't think we have a plan. Yet. They are information-gathering at the moment."

Carmella looked unimpressed, and they all went back to work.

There was another buzz.

"Oh!" shouted Penny. "This is marvellous, Tariq has seen someone post on social media about waking up and finding a scarecrow dressed in a top hat in their garden!"

"Fred Astaire!" said Izzy.

Penny opened her laptop and pulled up a map. "It was in a village called Horringer over by Bury St Edmunds. Obviously, we don't know when it fell into their garden, but at least it means Remi and Tariq are heading in the right direction."

"Tell me more about Remi," said Carmella. "He is on a birdwatching holiday here, is that correct? Why on earth did he agree to help with something so very absurd?"

"He and Penny have been doing goo-goo eyes at each other," said Izzy.

Penny sighed loudly. "Nobody even knows what that means, Izzy."

"Ah yes," said Carmella. "So he was your date for last night. I have seen you pull that expression, now that I come to think of it. I thought I saw it with the carpenter – is his name Aubrey? – but he's with the lady doctor, isn't he, so I must have been mistaken."

Penny could feel her cheeks turning crimson, so she picked up her phone, willing Tariq to send another message. When nothing appeared, she started running searches on various social media sites, looking for mentions of scarecrows or UFOs.

Izzy had spent the last few minutes walking around their workspaces, counting supplies and checking against tickets. She picked up a pen and started to make notes on the board.

"By my reckoning, we will need another seven heads, and six more body sticks of some sort. I think we can eke out the straw we have to stuff the remaining bodies, as long as we are a little bit frugal with it. It's the outfits that will be more challenging. Carmella has proved adept at making hats out of interfacing, but for Bob the Builder we probably need a genuine yellow hard hat. We have all been avoiding doing Ed Sheeran, because we need a decent wig, and probably a guitar to make it clear who he is. Actually, if we can find some toy guitars, we should get one for Keith Richards as well. We could do with a velvet curtain for Charles II's robe, and we need a doctor's coat and a stethoscope for the surgeon scarecrow."

"That list is not too bad," said Penny. "All things considered."

"You haven't started on Nemo," said Izzy with a sideways look at the ticket Penny had taken, "but I think we can make that from what we have in the shop."

"Give it to me," said Carmella, holding out a hand. "I'm on a roll with my interfacing creations. A fish face is like a sideways hat. I might run up a line of couture hats for my shop when all of this is over."

"What will make them couture, Carmella?" asked Penny.

"Oh, definitely the price tag," said Carmella with a smile.

Penny picked up her phone. "Tariq says they're just outside Cambridge and the trail is getting warm. There have been some sightings over that way. Tariq will send up his drone in the next twenty minutes or so when it gets fully light."

"How soon will the bakery open do you think?" Izzy asked. "We are all in desperate need of a sugary snack and frothy coffee to keep us going."

"Let's keep an eye out for any movement on Market Hill," said Penny. "If we see someone headed in there maybe we could plead with them to sell us something before official opening."

They all stared wistfully out of the window, willing the bakers to turn up to work and provide a delicious breakfast.

"Oh! Gather round, this should be interesting!" called Penny. "Tariq says he can share the video feed from his drone on a call with us, so we can see what they are seeing."

Tariq connected through on a video call. *"Hello from the two of us here in a car park!"* Tariq and Remi waved at the camera, from what looked like an empty car park in the early morning light.

"Good morning from the sewing shop!" said Penny and made sure they all waved back.

"*I will connect the drone feed to the call and then we will launch,*" said Tariq. "*The video from its camera will be what you see next.*"

Penny propped up the phone so that she, Izzy and Carmella could watch. It showed a dizzying perspective of Remi and Tariq being left on the ground and turning into barely visible specks as the drone headed up over what was presumably the city of Cambridge. Penny could see some of the grand old university buildings, although she didn't know what the layout of Cambridge looked like.

"What might we expect to see?" asked Izzy. "Do we know how far up the balloon might be?"

"*We've been chatting,*" said Remi, "*and we hope the balloon might have lost some gas with all the buffeting. At any rate, the weight of the scarecrows should keep it lower. We hope it will be within a couple of hundred feet at most, so visible from the ground.*"

"*That's why I don't want to go too high,*" added Tariq. "*I will do a search of the area at this height. We believe it's been seen over Cambridge within the past thirty minutes, so we are hopeful of finding it.*"

Penny was glued to the smooth rolling view of the city's rooftops. Every so often Tariq would make some adjustment and the angle or height would change slightly, but so far there had been nothing else in the sky apart from birds.

"How are you three holding up?" asked Remi. "You have worked all night, yes?"

"We have," said Penny. "But we've made amazing progress."

Izzy leaned over and whispered to Carmella. "See? Goo-goo eyes."

"Sorry—?" Remi started, but then Tariq cut across him.

"Look! I see something!"

The drone dropped down and all of them could see it too.

"It's the pig!" said Izzy. "And quite a few of the scarecrows."

"But nowhere near all of them," said Carmella.

"Signing off, so we can go and chase it now we have a position," said Tariq and the call ended.

The three women looked at each other. "Well it's in their hands now," said Penny.

"I didn't see Elvis in amongst the remaining ones," said Izzy in a small voice. "Of all the scarecrows I would have liked to recover, it's that one. Do you remember the work we put into it?"

"I do," said Penny, putting an arm round Izzy's shoulders.

"Come come," said Carmella. "It's not all bad news. I can see a light on in the bakery."

38

Izzy went out to try and make an early purchase from Wallertons. She came back empty-handed, but with the promise there would be a delivery to the shop as soon as the first batch of baked goods were ready.

"Izzy, the most amazing thing has happened!" Penny said as she walked through the door. "They have the balloon! Tariq and Remi have the balloon!"

"What? How on earth did they do that?"

"Would you believe it got tangled in a children's climbing frame? Look, here's a picture of Remi at the top of the slide. He's just about level with the pig's face!"

Penny showed her the photo.

"Whoa, that is an amazing picture! His smile looks just like the pig's smile. You do know that Tariq will explode if he can't share this with the world?"

"He has promised to keep it private. They are just

working out a way to get the pig back here. Tariq wants to tie it to the back of Remi's motorbike."

Izzy looked back and forth between Penny and Carmella. "You're not serious? They can't do that! Even if their combined weight is enough to keep the bike on the road, they would never be able to drag it all the way back to Fram without causing some sort of terrible accident."

"I think Remi has persuaded Tariq there are perhaps better options," said Penny.

"Did they find any of the scarecrows?" asked Izzy.

"Yes, they did. Quite a few have obviously been lost along the way, but they have Ed Sheeran, 'Freddie Mongrelly', Nemo and a couple of the other tricky ones."

"Not Elvis though?"

Penny shook her head sadly. "No. I'm so sorry Izzy. Carmella and I were just talking about the others. I asked Aubrey if he might be up for doing us a big favour with his van, and he's popping in when he can. If he can go and meet Remi and Tariq, he could fetch the remaining scarecrows back here."

"And talk them out of any daft ideas of towing the balloon back too, I hope. I'm sticking the kettle on. Some strong coffee is needed if we're to power on through the day."

"What kind of beans do you use?" said Carmella. "I only use hand-roasted Guatemalan beans."

"Yeah, I don't think we've got hand-roasted anything. If it's from our kitchenette, you'll be lucky if it's not instant coffee."

"People and their finnicky preferences in coffee," Penny mused.

"I'm not finnicky," said Carmella. "I just have taste."

Izzy was carrying the coffee downstairs when she heard Penny shout: "I've found them!"

"Found who? The scarecrows? Elvis?" Izzy clattered into the shop.

"No, not Elvis, sorry," said Penny. "The women."

"What women?"

Penny had her work laptop open on the counter. On the screen was a local newspaper article and picture of an array of smiling uniformed figures.

"Chief Constable hands out commendations," Izzy read aloud.

"What's this about?" said Carmella.

"Something we've been looking into," said Penny.

The image was of an awards ceremony for police officers from what turned out to be the Norfolk constabulary, each holding little plaque awards. Penny's finger went to the picture caption underneath. Izzy scanned and saw *PC Eve Bennefer* and *PC Ulrike Merrison* among the names.

"Eve Bennefer and Ulrike Merrison," said Izzy.

"And there's a PC Rebecca George too," said Penny. "Becky. The woman at Remi's hostel."

"She's relevant?"

"She's been watching Pageant House for more than a week."

Izzy frowned. "Three police officers. All visited Pageant House."

"Possibly ex-police. This article is twelve years old. And that—" Penny put her finger on the screen "—that's Eve, the woman who fell off the wall. She's changed a bit since then."

The woman's hair was not unlike that of the woman Izzy had seen at the bottom of the stairs, but even though the dead woman had been on her front, her face turned away, Izzy knew her Eve Bennefer was not that woman. She scanned the image until she saw a far more likely candidate and checked the caption.

"Do the names match the people left to right?" she said. "Or is it the people stood behind and then the ones stood in front." There were more than a dozen people in the picture. After staring for ten seconds, Izzy concluded one couldn't match names to faces. "Police officers, huh?"

"Two of them dead, now."

"What are you two wittering about?" said Carmella, who having sniffed and tasted her coffee, had put it to one side.

"Policewomen," said Izzy. "People we've met, sort of. We've found them in this police commendation picture."

"What are they getting commendations for?" said Carmella.

"Is it relevant?" said Izzy, but Penny was already searching. "Hmmm. PC Bennefer. Rescuing a rough sleeper from a fire at ... hmmm."

"Hmmm?"

"Oh. Hang on. That's ... weird."

She showed Izzy the screen again. It was another news article. Izzy could tell from the clunking webpage layout that this too was from some years ago. The central image was of the smouldering ruins of a hotel-like building set back on green lawns.

"That's the Hunterton Casino," said Penny.

Izzy didn't understand until she saw the jester logo on the end of the partially destroyed sign over the veranda entrance.

"*That* casino?" said Izzy, shocked.

"That casino."

"What casino?" said Carmella. "You two talk in half-sentences and riddles."

Penny had a wide-eyed looked of disbelief on her face even as she explained to Carmella. "Weeks ago, Monty found a bag of cash in the street."

"I recall," said Carmella tartly.

"You said we'd made it up to get our faces in the paper."

"I did."

"Except we didn't. No one came to claim it and we couldn't return it to the owners because they'd gone out of business." She pointed a finger at the image on the screen. "That's the logo. That's the casino."

"And this is exciting because...?"

Izzy tried to put what they definitely knew into words. "There was a fire at a casino twelve years ago. Penny and Monty found a bag of money from the casino here in Fram. And now, in the space of a week, three of the police officers who were present at the fire have shown their faces in Fram."

"And two of them are dead," said Penny. "Becky George was watching Eve's house for a week. Ulrike's car is in Eve's driveway. Eve is dead. And I guess the other woman is Ulrike Merrison."

"Did this Becky kill them?" said Izzy.

"But why?"

"Money? Eve did buy that house with cash."

Izzy looked at the image of the burned out casino. Possible scenarios lined up in her mind. She was about to give voice to the most obvious of them when the door to the shop opened.

39

Aubrey appeared at the same time as the fresh pastries from Wallertons. He sat down and listened as Penny and Izzy explained what had happened with the scarecrows. He kept glancing across at Carmella, as if expecting her to bite at any moment.

"None of you have slept since yesterday?" he asked.

They all shook their heads.

"And you have re-made all of these scarecrows?" He nodded at the line-up of completed and semi-completed scarecrows propped against the fabric display shelving, as if they were queuing to be let out.

"Yes." Penny nodded. "We really did. I can't quite believe it, but we did."

"And you've what, been eating onions to keep yourselves awake?" he asked, sniffing the air, confused.

Carmella laughed at that. She laughed so long and hard

that Izzy started to wonder if there was something the matter with her.

"I can't even smell the onions anymore!" laughed Carmella. "It's done something weird to my brain being locked up in here for so long. I have forgotten how to smell onion, and I have forgotten that I really don't like any of you."

"Rude," said Aubrey with a frown, realising he was included. "Anyway, I'll get going in a moment, meet up with Remi and Tariq and help them bring back the runaway pig. Hopefully I can get back to Fram before Stuart realises I'm gone."

"Oh, Carmella has arranged for a pig-related distraction so that he and Arabella will be out all day competing against Frank Mountjoy," said Penny.

"Nice. That does sound like something that would keep him busy." Aubrey stood to leave. "I'll message when I am on my way back, then we might as well use the van to get all these other scarecrows up to the castle before Stuart gets back."

"Thanks Aubrey! As always, we are indebted to you," said Penny with a wave.

"You might want to move them out of sight," he called as he left. "It's going to look a bit odd if people look in here and see all the scarecrows that should be up at the castle."

"He's right! Where can we put them?" Izzy popped the remains of a croissant into her mouth and gave it some thought. "If we put them up the stairs they won't be too far to carry, but they will not be so obvious from outside."

"Do you mean one on each step, as if they are all waiting in line to make their big entrance?" asked Penny.

"Yeah. Why not?"

Penny and Carmella exchanged a glance.

"Allow me," said Carmella, gesturing at Penny to indicate she would explain. "If the events of the last twenty four hours have taught us anything, it's that you *don't* set up an obvious accident waiting to happen. If you stand your scarecrows up like dominoes, waiting to pile up in a mess at the bottom of the stairs, I can confidently predict you will achieve domino mess in no time at all."

Izzy nodded. "I see your point. Maybe we need to split them up for safety. We can assemble them into casual groups, with a sheet of fabric draped over each one."

They did just that. Izzy was confident they had at least made the shop navigable for customers, although there was still the lingering smell of onions.

Izzy texted Marcin for a little moral support.

Things are tense, but I hope soon all will be resolved. Send me uplifting thoughts!

Waiting for the return of Aubrey, Remi and Tariq, the mood in the shop became slightly strained. As the frantic making of the night-time hours gave way to a nervous anticipation of moving the scarecrows up to the castle, all three women found themselves overwhelmed with tiredness. Carmella stalked around the shop and found fault with everything she picked up, while Penny tried to make lists to organise what needed to happen next, but wasn't sure where to start.

We will have pierogi later. Maybe after you have a nap

"Ooh, yum. *Pierogi!*" said Izzy out loud as she read the message.

"What?" snapped Carmella.

"Oh! They're here!" shouted Penny. "Thank goodness."

Aubrey's van pulled up, with Remi's motorcycle just behind. As all three men came in through the door, Izzy ran to the window to check the pig balloon had not been tethered somewhere noticeable.

"Hello! We are very glad to see you!" said Penny to all three of them, although Izzy tried to work out what the pecking order might be between Remi and Aubrey in terms of Penny's enthusiasm.

"I think we have achieved everything that we needed to do," said Remi, modestly.

"Tell me! How did you handle the balloon?" asked Penny. She too was peering outside, trying to see where it might be.

"It was actually pretty easy in the end," said Tariq. "Remi had the genius idea of calling the company Stuart hired it from. They told us how to deflate it, so it's in the back of Aubrey's van."

"But what about re-inflating it?" asked Penny.

Aubrey shrugged. "The company, Suffolk Blimps, will come and do that for us up at the castle. They're offering some big prizes for the competition anyway and are just happy to help out. I'll just tell Stuart that the balloon looked like it was going down so I called them out."

"Incredible! Just incredible," said Penny. "When the dust has settled, I will buy you all a proper drink, but for now we need to get the scarecrows in the van and up to the castle."

40

Penny slammed the door on Aubrey's van as the last of the scarecrows were loaded in. She looked around the market place, but it was still early enough that there were few people about.

"Izzy and I will close the shop and meet you up at the castle in a few minutes," she said.

Aubrey set off, with Tariq in the passenger seat.

"This has been a most peculiar adventure," said Remi, thoughtfully.

"You must think we're all quite mad," said Penny.

"For sure," he grinned, "but only in a good way."

They walked slowly up the street towards the castle. Izzy seemed quiet.

"Are you thinking about your dad's Elvis suit?" Penny asked.

Izzy nodded. "I need to go and break the news to him at

some point. That was a lovely outfit. The jacket was so magnificently gaudy."

"By the way, I have not seen Becky," said Remi.

"Becky?" said Izzy.

"Your mention of gaudy jackets reminded me. Sorry. When Penny came to the accommodation, waving a jacket and hoping to see Becky. She has not returned to the house since then."

"Perhaps she has left?" Penny suggested, but Remi shook his head.

"She has left a car on the driveway and a pair of boots by the door."

"We could really do with talking to her," said Izzy, "if we are to understand what happened at Pageant House."

"Pageant House?"

They stopped near the community hall and Penny pointed at the house on the opposite side of the road to the ice cream shop. "Pageant House. It's a very odd story."

"Oh, I like odd stories," said Remi.

"Twelve years ago—"

"Oh, it's an old odd story," he smiled.

"Twelve years ago there were three women who were officers in the Norfolk police: Eve Bennefer, Ulrike Merrison and Becky George. We saw a photo of them being given bravery awards. This old casino in Great Yarmouth burned down and they, at least one of them, rescued a rough sleeper from the building as it burned. Recently, Eve Bennefer bought that house, Pageant House, and employed Aubrey to repaint it top to bottom."

"Don't forget the bag," said Izzy.

"Also, a few weeks ago, our dog Monty found a bag of cash here in Framlingham."

"Bag of cash?" said Remi.

"Just a bit in it. Hundreds not thousands."

"Oh, to have a few hundred pounds more than I do."

"The point is the bag was marked with the jester logo used by the Hunterton Casino."

"I'm not sure I understand," said Remi.

"Nor do we," said Penny. "Now, for the past week or more, Becky George, former copper, has been watching Pageant House from a table in the ice cream shop."

"Meanwhile, Ulrike Merrison's car has been parked in the driveway there," said Izzy. There was no car there now. "I guess the police took it away."

"So, the three police officers are here," said Remi.

"Or were."

"Aubrey went to the house on Monday to continue decorating," said Penny. "Eve was there, she got shirty with him and sent him away. Later that evening, Eve went to the castle. You took a photo showing her on the castle wall with someone only minutes before she fell and died."

"That is terrible," said Remi.

"What's weird," said Izzy, "apart from the scream—"

"What's weird about the scream?" said Penny.

"Did I not tell you? I'll come back to that. What's odd is that when she fell, the two people who were already up there, Aubrey and Monica, didn't see anyone come past them. Which is impossible."

"Don't believe Izzy when she tells you a ghost did it," Penny put in. "What we do know is, shortly after, Becky

George dumped her distinctive jacket in a bag of donated clothes outside the charity shop door."

"Why?" said Remi.

Penny shrugged. "Oh, if I can speculate, I'd say that if she had pushed Eve off the wall, then perhaps a clever ex-copper might decide to get rid of any clothes she was wearing that night in case someone recognised her. Or if she thought there might be DNA evidence on them."

"A good thought," said Izzy.

"And now you think Becky killed Eve," said Remi.

"Except," said Izzy heavily, "on Thursday evening, Aubrey got an irate phone message from Eve—"

"The dead woman?"

"Exactly, telling him to come to her house. I went with him."

"Izzy is a licensed Ghostbuster," said Penny.

"Really?" said Remi.

"No," said Izzy.

"Ah, the famous British sarcasm."

"I went with him, the front door was open, and there was a dead woman at the foot of the stairs."

"Really?"

"Really."

"Who was it?"

"Well, it can't have been Eve because Eve was already dead. Aubrey had identified her body."

"But Eve had made the phone call?"

"So, Aubrey believed."

"It's the strangest thing," said Penny.

Remi grunted to himself. "I do not think that is the strangest thing."

"You don't?"

"No. All of this is curious and odd, but the strangest thing of all is that your dog, Monty, should happen to find a bag of money from that casino here in the streets of Framlingham."

"You're not wrong," said Penny. "Come on, we'd best get these scarecrows set up."

Izzy hesitated. "Maybe I need to go break the bad news to dad, now."

Penny nodded in understanding. "Why don't you take an hour now?" she said. "I can sort out the scarecrows with Carmella and the others. There's no point in putting it off."

"Thanks. I will do that." Izzy left, her shoulders slumped.

41

Remi entered the castle with Penny. Aubrey had drawn his van inside and was unloading the remaining scarecrows. Carmella was spacing them out and considering the spaces they might go in. Tariq had stepped away to take more photos.

"You know, you can never share these photos," Penny reminded him sternly.

"It's just for us," Tariq said. "We could have one of them whatchermacallits – a tontine."

"A what?" said Aubrey.

"A deal where the last surviving person keeps all the profits," said Remi.

"How would that work?" said Carmella.

"I'd take the photos and whichever of us is still alive in, say, thirty years' time, can sell our story to the press," said Tariq, excited by the idea.

"That feels morbid, somehow," said Penny.

"I think it sounds fun," said Carmella. "Last woman standing and all that."

Penny felt an urge to point out that Carmella was, by some years, the oldest person present, but held her tongue. She turned her attention to the scarecrows.

"Let's lay them all out in the place we're going to fasten them, so we can make sure we've spaced them out correctly."

She grabbed the new Frida Kahlo scarecrow, then she realised Carmella had grabbed Elphaba from *Wicked*. They both sprinted for the prized location at the focal point of the space.

"And here we are again, right where the entire calamity began," said Penny. "We should do something different this time."

"Yes, we should," said Carmella.

Penny cast around for a decent compromise. "Why don't we find a scarecrow that we find non-threatening, like Dustin over there from *Stranger Things*. We put him in the middle and ours go either side."

"I have no idea who Dustin is, but I suppose that might work."

They arranged the rest of the scarecrows, and Aubrey oversaw the re-inflation of the balloon. Soon it was bobbing overhead again, securely anchored to a new fixing point.

"Do the British always have big pig balloons at scarecrow festivals?" said Remi.

"No. That's just part of the Fram madness," said Penny.

Within the hour, all the scarecrows were in place. They weren't the same scarecrows as before, and it was highly unlikely any of the creators would be fooled into thinking these doppelgangers were their originals, but there were scarecrows enough to entertain visitors and, hopefully, help raise funds for the Community Change charity.

"It looks good," said Aubrey.

"This horrible ordeal is finally at an end," said Carmella, in a voice so melodramatic that she might as well have put the back of a hand to her forehead and swooned. "I shall retire to a long bath and a face mask, returning tomorrow for the adjudication and my much-deserved prize."

As Carmella walked out through the high gate, Penny clapped her hands.

"Right, boys and girls! It's time to pack up and vamoose, and pretend we were never here! Tariq, that includes you, so stop snapping!" She walked back over the moat bridge with Tariq and Remi. "I owe you both a debt of thanks."

"You kidding?" said Tariq. "This has been fun."

"But we owe you a pint at least." She turned to Remi and on a whim reached out and tugged at a crease in his lapel. "And you... I think I might owe you a dinner."

"That would be very nice," he said. His eyes met hers, and she had no idea what to do with the feeling that look sent through her.

"A pint will be fine for me," said Tariq.

"I am going to the mere to see what I might still spot today with my beautiful calash," said Remi. "But I will call on you at the shop at ... shall we say seven o'clock?"

"Seven o'clock," said Penny.

Remi waved a farewell and he and Tariq walked down the driveway towards the town.

Aubrey carefully manoeuvred his van through the gateway and got out to lock up.

There was a shout. "Wait! Wait!"

Aubrey and Penny turned to look.

Izzy came cycling up the drive on her yarn-bombed bicycle, narrowly avoiding Remi and Tariq as she passed. It initially looked like she was giving a piggyback to a man in a superhero cape, then she saw it was nothing of the sort.

Izzy had an Elvis scarecrow draped over her shoulder.

"Penny! Penny! You'll never guess what's happened!"

"Where on earth did you get that from?" Penny asked. "It's your dad's actual original one, isn't it?"

Izzy skidded to a halt. "Can you believe that it landed in someone's garden and they phoned my dad to go and collect it?"

"They knew it was his?" Aubrey was incredulous.

"Well, he is the number one Elvis impersonator in the area," said Izzy.

"That is the cherry on top of the cake. I think we can call this a win."

With Aubrey's help, they installed Elvis in the line.

"Things don't just turn up, do they?" said Izzy.

"Hmm?" said Penny, stamping in the dirt around the base of the Elvis scarecrow.

"Like Elvis here. He didn't just magically appear in that garden. If you could go back and follow the balloon, you'd see with the wind patterns and wotnot exactly how it ended up where it was."

"I suppose."

"So, it's like Remi said, that bag of money must have come from somewhere."

"Bag of money?" said Aubrey.

"You know," said Penny. "The one Monty found."

"Ah, Treasure Dog, the Indiana Jones of the corgi world."

"Well, yes."

"If that money came from a burned down casino in Great Yarmouth then it got here somehow."

"Eve Bennefer is the obvious answer," said Izzy.

"Obvious?" said Aubrey.

"Two things we know that had been at the casino: Eve Bennefer and that bag."

Elvis was securely in place. Penny moved towards the gate.

"Monty found the bag this end of town, but it was some minutes before I noticed he had it."

"Could it have come from Pageant House?" said Aubrey.

"Well, he didn't go inside, if that's what you mean."

"This was two, three weeks ago, wasn't it? So, Eve would have been on her holiday."

"Right, because she was deliberately away while you were doing the decorating."

"A Mediterranean cruise from Southampton if I recall. The *MS Emeraldine*."

"You remember the ship name?" said Izzy.

"Only because it's also the name of particularly sickly shade of expensive paint. If you ever end up in Stuart Dinktrout's bedroom, you'll see it and wonder how anyone could pick it."

"If I ever end up in Stuart Dinktrout's bedroom, there will be plenty of other questions on my mind," said Penny.

They were outside the castle now and Aubrey, with an obvious sense of relief at putting the clandestine shenanigans behind him, locked the gate.

Izzy was staring at Pageant House. "Is there—? No."

"Is there what?" said Penny.

"I'm just thinking... If Eve Bennefer was away on her jolly cruise and the bag of money appeared in the street outside her house..."

"Yes?"

"Well, the only person to go into the house during that time was you, Aubrey."

He frowned at her. "You're suggesting I ... I don't even know what you're suggesting. That I went into her house, found her 'souvenir' bag of casino cash and flung it into the street?"

"Hmmm. Souvenir bag of casino cash," said Izzy. "We're all thinking the same thing, right?"

"No one is ever thinking the same thing as you, Izzy," said Penny.

"She stole that bag, right?" said Aubrey.

Izzy nodded. "Woman was in casino; years later, woman is in Fram. So is a bag of cash from said casino."

"She stole it," said Penny. "Bizarrely, that is the most obvious explanation."

Aubrey tutted at himself. "There's something I should tell you..."

Izzy looked at him. "Is there?"

"No, not *should* tell, but I want to tell you – even though I shouldn't."

"Oh?"

"Because if I tell you there will be more hijinks and, as the last few days has shown, hijinks do not necessarily lead to good places."

"Right? What is it?"

He delved into his overall pocket and pulled out a single key on a plastic keyring. "I still have the key to Pageant House that Eve gave me."

"Oh," said Penny.

"If we think she had stolen casino loot in her house we could…" He was unwilling to end the sentence.

"We could go look," said Izzy.

Penny nodded slowly. "It might be my sleep-deprived brain talking, but that sounds like a brilliant idea."

42

Aubrey parked his van at the bottom of the castle drive and Izzy walked down to meet him. She looked at Pageant House with a feeling she eventually recognised as trepidation. The dark windows on the top floor were like gaunt, hollow eyes.

"Last time we went in there, we found a body," she said.

"I don't think finding one body on your one visit is enough to establish a pattern," said Penny, helpfully.

Aubrey approached the door, key in hand.

"What's that?" said Penny.

"What's what?" said Izzy.

There was a plastic blob fixed to the wooden upright of the nearby rose arch. The plastic blob had a lens in it.

"It's a camera," said Aubrey. He bent to inspect it, then looked in the direction it was facing. "Watching the door."

"Eve had CCTV?" said Penny.

"Usually, people have very prominent CCTV or doorbell cameras. Half the point is you want people to know they're being watched." He tugged, and it came away on a sticky strip.

Izzy gasped. "Ah, the police! It's a police camera, guarding the crime scene."

Aubrey twitched his face doubtfully. "Might be cheaper than an actual copper, but I can't see the police going to this much bother."

Aubrey tried to put the camera back. It wouldn't stick. He placed it on the ground then unlocked the door. "Hello!" he called as he pushed it open. "Aubrey Jones here! Decorator! Just come to collect my things!"

"And who exactly are you calling out to?" said Penny, coming in behind him. "Eve Bennefer is dead."

"I used to think that too," he said. "Then she phoned me."

They walked through the kitchen. Aubrey's decorating gear remained on the counter, gathering dust. Izzy stopped in the hallway. She had stood in the hallway of Pageant House before, yet seeing it now without a body on the floor by the stairs, it felt like an unfamiliar place.

"You painted all of this?" said Penny.

"Top to bottom," said Aubrey. "Literally. Best way to work. Did the upstairs first."

"I like the beige colour," she said, waving a hand at the walls above the stairs.

"Elephant's Breath."

"Very nice."

"So," said Izzy, rousing herself from staring at the spot

where the body had been, "we're working on the theory that she had a bag of money from the casino and which, at some point, for some reason, went from this house into the street, where Monty found it."

"Even though she'd really not moved in?" said Aubrey. "She'd barely bought the house before calling me in to decorate then going on an extended cruise. Look, everything's still in boxes."

He led the way upstairs. Halfway up, at the sound of a small creak from above, he froze. "You hear that?"

"It's not a ghost," said Penny firmly.

"I didn't say it was. Old house."

"Bats," said Izzy.

"Pigeons," suggested Aubrey.

"Bees."

"But not a ghost," Penny confirmed, as positive as before.

There were five doors off the upstairs landing, and a hatch to the attic above. Aubrey was right: the rooms on the first floor were mostly furnished with packing boxes.

"There's not actually that many of them," said Izzy.

"What do you mean?" said Penny.

"I had as many as this when I moved in with Marcin, and Eve Bennefer was older than me."

Penny smiled. "The accumulation of stuff with age? You are something of a hoarder, Izzy."

"I consider myself to be quite unmaterialistic," she replied, mildly affronted.

"A thousand and one craft projects you refuse to throw out."

"They don't count. They're not things. Art does not count as things."

Aubrey stepped into the large master bedroom. "This was the first room I painted." He gestured at the boxes and the only item of furniture, an old chest of drawers. "Had to lunk things around the room in order to clear space to paint."

Izzy went to the window and looked down, directly onto the pavement of the street outside.

"Was this window ever open?" she said.

"Sorry?" said Aubrey.

It was an old sash cord window. It had been painted shut at some point in the past, but there were crumbly flakes in the gap where the window, reopened, had pulled the painted sections apart.

"You opened this window while you painted?" she said.

"Sure," said Aubrey. "Aired room, dries quicker."

Penny stepped forward. "You think … you think Monty and I found that bag because it fell from this window?"

"I didn't just open a window, find a bag of cash and toss it out," said Aubrey. "I would have remembered."

"So, what did you do?" said Penny. "Nice colour scheme again. Pink can be sickly at times, but this is nice."

"Thanks. I think."

Izzy crouched to inspect the floor. There were light scuff marks on the bare floorboards beneath the window. "You moved something from here?"

"I didn't," he said.

Izzy tracked the scuff marks to the chest of drawers. It had a curved front and a polished walnut finish. She tried the drawers. Most of them were stiff, and she could tell they were empty even before she'd opened them. The top drawer was locked, a dark little keyhole at its centre. "This was in front of the window, Aubrey."

"No, actually," he said. "It was there. I had to move it across to get to the wall behind."

Izzy locked eyes with Penny. Together they moved to either side of the chest of drawers. They were about to move it when Penny said, "Wait a moment, this is broken."

With a grunt, she pivoted her end round. The front of the chest might have been stylish, vintage and highly polished, but the rear was just a simple piece of wooden board, crudely tacked on with nails. Around the top and sides the thin board had come loose and was hanging like a flap.

"Oh, there's a possibility," said Izzy.

"Unlikely," said Penny.

"But a possibility," said Izzy.

"Would someone tell me what you're going on about?" said Aubrey.

"Let's imagine," said Izzy, "that Eve Bennefer did, for some reason, have a bag of cash from the casino and she'd, I dunno, either stored it in the drawers or hidden it behind that back panel."

"Right...?"

"Along comes Aubrey, Mr Painter-Man, and he moves the chest of drawers so he can paint the wall."

"Here," said Penny, gesturing to a chipped spot in the window frame and a corresponding fleck of white paint on the panel at the back of the drawers. "You moved this over to the open window. Maybe the back was already coming off, maybe you loosened it when you pushed it against the window frame."

"And the bag of money just fell out the back?" said Aubrey.

"Out of the window and onto the pavement for a little dog to find," said Izzy.

"Improbable."

"But possible," she said.

43

Penny considered the whole room and tried to imagine the scene. "Did Eve Bennefer say anything particular about this chest of drawers? Did she act funny or anything when she showed you round?"

"She never got to show me round. We just chatted, gave me the brief – it was very simple really, just a paint job – then she dropped the keys through my letter box before she went on her holiday."

Penny frowned. "But ... you did *see* her, though? I mean, you did actually meet her before she went?"

"No. I told you. She called me. On the phone. She talked me through it. A big job but a simple one. Repaint everything. She had her boat to catch."

"But you identified her body at the castle."

"Well, I'd met her by that time," he said. "That morning. I went round and she'd come back."

There was wild energy in Penny as she absorbed this, a quiet fury. "What did she say to you?" she demanded.

"When I met her?"

"When you came into the house on Monday morning. You opened the door because you weren't expecting her to be here, and you saw her. What exactly was said?"

Aubrey spluttered a little under the pressure. "I, er, I apologised automatically, because I was surprised. She told me it wasn't convenient for me to be there."

"Those were her first words?"

"Yes."

"So, it was 'Sorry, Ms Bennefer, didn't mean to surprise you' and then 'It's not convenient right now, Aubrey, get out'?"

"Well, not quite like that."

"Then how?" she insisted.

Izzy was frowning too, clearly unaware of what Penny was driving at.

"I, um, it was more like I came in and saw her in the hallway," said Aubrey, "and she was as surprised to see me as I was her. I apologised, pretty much as you say, and said I just needed to get finished in the kitchen. She was just staring at me – like she'd forgotten I was still working there."

"And then?"

"Then she sort of got over her surprise and told me she didn't care, and didn't I know to knock, and no, I couldn't work there that day."

Penny exhaled deeply. "It's flaming sardines!" she said.

"Is it?" said Izzy, keen to be involved.

"Different things get called sardines based on where you find them. Remi and I were discussing it over dinner."

"Right...?" said Aubrey.

"You called her Ms Bennefer," said Penny. "Why?"

He frowned. "Because it was?"

She shook her head. "You called her Ms Bennefer because you found her in this house. You found a woman in this house, and because she was here, you assumed she was Eve Bennefer. Some sort of Norfolk accent, I'm guessing."

"A little twang," Aubrey conceded.

"And then at the castle, the woman who fell, you recognised her as the same woman. Ergo it must be Eve Bennefer."

"Ergo," said Izzy, impressed with the word.

"So, it wasn't Eve Bennefer?" said Aubrey.

Izzy clicked her fingers. "Ulrike Merrison. The woman whose car was in the drive."

"Right," said Penny. "She came in here. Broke in. Let's assume police officers, or ex-police officers, know their way around a lock. Then you come in and surprise her."

"She pretended to be Eve Bennefer," said Aubrey.

"She didn't need to. You made all the assumptions."

"You're making me sound like an idiot."

"Not at all," said Penny, trying to reinject some calm into her tone. "You're not. What you are is someone who assumes the best in others and quite reasonably thinks that if you find a woman in a house, then both the woman and the house belong to one another."

"But I told the police," he said, a note of worry in his voice.

"An honest mistake."

"And that explains the voicemail message," said Izzy. "Eve hadn't come home early from her holiday at all. She came home as planned on Wednesday. She had no idea what had gone on at the castle."

"Yes," Penny nodded. "She came home and found the decorating job unfinished."

"I thought she was dead!" protested Aubrey.

"You did, but all she saw was unfinished work, so she phoned you. She left that message."

"Oh, my goodness," he said, clutching his chest. "So there's no ghosts?"

"Never were," said Penny.

"Well…" Izzy began.

Penny held up a finger to silence her. "No ghosts at all."

Aubrey gathered some of his decorating equipment, for the sake of appearances if nothing else, and the three of them left the house.

"There's still so much that doesn't make sense about this," he said as they stepped outside.

"A lot," Penny agreed, "but I need to go home. I am being collected for a dinner date."

"Another? So soon?" said Izzy, pretending to be scandalised.

"And I imagine with the zero sleep I've had there's the biggest rings under my eyes. Some power napping and emergency prepping might be required."

"Are we not opening the shop today?" said Izzy. "I mean, to customers?"

"Do you want to?" said Penny. "Or would you perhaps

like to spend the rest of Saturday catching up on the rest you lost?"

Izzy gave it considerable thought. "I suppose people can cope without sewing supplies for one day."

"Yes, I reckon so."

While Aubrey went to the van, Penny walked back to the shop, with Izzy wheeling her bike beside her, then the two cousins parted. Monty bounded up to greet Penny as she returned.

"Oh, little boy, the shortest of walks for you I think," she said. "Then an afternoon of doing very little."

Monty seemed content enough with a wander round the edges of the church graveyard and a sniff at familiar landmarks. They returned to the shop, where the closing and locking of the shop door to the whole world outside was an almost physical relief to Penny.

"We are done for the day, Monty," she declared and then looked at the clock. "Until seven at least."

She put down food for the little corgi and refreshed his water before going upstairs to her little apartment rooms. The heat of the day had made the rooms hot and stifling, but Penny propped open a window and let a flow of air and the sounds of the Saturday market drift through.

She poured herself a cooling drink of juice from the fridge and sat in her favourite upright armchair by the window. It had been a crazy few days, both in terms of scarecrow nonsense, and the most peculiar affair of Eve Bennefer and the woman on the castle walls.

A thought crossed her mind and she woke her phone to search for any news stories regarding the Hunterton Casino at Great Yarmouth. The place had burned to the ground twelve years ago, but there were some news stories on the internet dating back before then.

The most pertinent of the news articles, at least in Penny's mind, was about how the casino had come to be closed and ultimately abandoned. Crown court reports weren't huge on details, but there had clearly been some scandal surrounding the place, apparently involving links between the owners and organised crime gangs, and the general manager being sentenced for embezzling funds from the casino itself.

"Interesting," she murmured.

There was sound of the fruit and veg man in the market outside hawking his wares, and a dog barking in response. Quite possibly Old McGillicuddy. Penny closed her eyes and tried to imagine what the dodgy business at the casino had to do with the three police women.

44

Izzy woke up at her normal time on Sunday morning, around quarter to seven.

"I expected you might sleep longer, given that you missed a whole night's sleep," said Marcin, handing her a cup of tea.

"Sleep never seems to work that way for me. I wish it would," said Izzy. "Anyway, I think I have been fortified by *pierogi*."

"They are known to cure all ills," said Marcin with a modest shrug. "And you did eat a great many of them. So today is the judging day for the scarecrows?"

"It is!" said Izzy. "I will be there to make sure the Frambeat Gazette gets everything it needs to report on the story. But mainly I will be there to make sure no more disasters strike the scarecrows."

"I would like to see these scarecrows," said Marcin. "I will come too."

The two of them went to church that morning and then called in on Penny. The door to Cozy Craft was locked. Izzy let herself in. The shop was quiet. On the doormat was a sheet of sketch paper with a somewhat cartoonish drawing of Remi de Smet and a speech bubble saying, *I am so sorry!*.

Izzy put the sheet on the counter and went to the foot of the stairs. "Penny! Are you in?"

There was the scratch of little claws on floorboards and Monty came scampering down to greet her. This was followed ten seconds later by the sight of Penny's bleary face peering into view, her hair all messed up and tangled.

"What time is?" she asked.

"Gone half eleven," said Izzy.

"Oh, heck! Give me a minute."

Within ten minutes, Penny was downstairs, looking far more respectable and ready for the day. Marcin was in the middle of the shop, teaching Monty to fall down dead when shot with a pretend finger-gun.

"I slept so much!" said Penny, then groaned. "I just sat down for five minutes to rest my eyes. I was meant to be going out for dinner with Remi. Oh, he must hate me."

Izzy showed her the sketch drawing on the counter.

"He's sorry? Why's he sorry? I must have been fast asleep up there while he was knocking on the door. I'm an idiot."

"You stayed awake for two whole days," said Izzy.

"I had the weirdest dreams about pigs."

"Pigs?" said Marcin.

"Pigs. Arabella and Grenville – that's Stuart and Frank's pigs. They were having a race on the sand, then started arguing over who should have the prize and I had to help them, except I was dressed like Ginger Rogers. Ostrich feathers everywhere."

"So the pigs were arguing?"

Penny blinked, as though still trying to dispel her sleepy brain fog. "They were Stuart and Frank too. You know how dreams are." She held up her phone. "Carmella's even sent me a text saying how much fun Frank and Stuart had at the pig races yesterday."

"The pig races that Carmella invented and that nobody else went to?" Izzy asked. She turned to explain to Marcin. "We had to get Stuart Dinktrout out of the way to stop him realising his large inflatable pig had gone missing."

"Of course you did," said Marcin with a shrug. "Just another day in the life of Izzy and Penny."

"Yes. Well, anyway, Carmella – who at any other time seems to exist only to pour scorn on everything we do – turned out to be a mastermind at scheming. She created a piggy diversion that kept Stuart and Frank out of Fram for the entire day."

"And now she is Penny's new best friend because she texts her with all of the updates," said Marcin, deadpan.

"Oh no, she still hates us and everything we stand for, apparently," said Penny, waggling her phone. "But we have a shared interest in covering up the scarecrow mishaps which we jointly caused."

They walked slowly up to the castle. There was a light but steady stream of people from the town also heading that way.

"I looked up that casino last night," said Penny.

"Oh?"

"Embezzled funds, links to organised crime. It occurred to me that maybe Eve or Ulrike or Becky, or maybe all three of them, found that bag of cash when they were there. When it burned down."

"You think whatever's happened is an argument over stolen loot?"

"It would make a lot of sense."

As they approached the entrance to the scarecrow festival, they were channelled through a path formed of vendors and stalls, selling scarecrow related merchandise and raising funds for local charities.

"Look at all of these straw hats!" said Penny pointing at a market stall. "These would have been very handy when we were doing our re-build."

"They do dog ones," said Izzy, pointing. "You should get one for Monty!"

Penny bought a tiny straw hat for Monty, who posed for a picture and then trotted on, knowing that all eyes were on him.

"There's Tariq, taking pictures of the scarecrows," said Penny.

"Your Nanna Lem and her boyfriend are over there," said Marcin.

Nanna Lem and Glenmore had stopped in front of the scarecrow versions of Fred and Ginger. Izzy looked at their faces, and nudged Penny.

There was no question of them lying about what had happened, because Penny immediately went bright red. Their deception had already been uncovered.

45

Nanna Lem gave her granddaughters a wry and knowing smile. "Hello girls. Marcin, how are you?" She took Marcin by the arm and leaned into him. "I expect you have nothing to do with whatever has gone on here. It's got Izzy and Penny written all over it. It also stinks of onions around here, but maybe *that* isn't their fault."

Marcin looked panicked for a moment, not sure whether he was being asked to confess.

"It's not what it looks like," said Izzy.

Glenmore turned so that he could glare more effectively at Izzy. "Not what it looks like? I'm not even sure what it's supposed to look like! Doppelganger scarecrows is what it looks like. Hastily made ones, at that! You think we would fail to recognise them after a day's absence?"

Izzy gave a little shrug. "Huh. Well, in that case it probably *is* what it looks like. What I meant is that we have a very good reason, and we will explain the whole thing to you. You might even laugh, because it's quite funny."

Izzy gave a small laugh by way of demonstration, but Glenmore continued to look deeply unimpressed.

"Shall we go and get a cup of tea so that Penny and Izzy can explain to us?" said Nanna Lem.

They found a tent where they could sit inside. There were familiar faces at several tables, so Izzy steered a path through all of them, finding the quietest possible corner. Tea and several slices of thick Victoria sponge were procured for them to enjoy.

Penny explained everything, with Izzy chipping in to add extra detail or colour as needed.

"So, Carmella Mountjoy sent them off on a wild goose chase for the day?" Nanna Lem hooted with glee.

"Shush Nanna!" hissed Penny.

Even Glenmore had smiled at the fake pig competition, but his eyes narrowed again as he realised something. "That hat and tux were rentals! What on earth will I do about that? It will cost me a fortune to replace them!"

There was a light cough from nearby.

"Tariq!" said Izzy, turning. "Getting some good pictures?"

"Yep. And that's not all I've got." He whipped his hands from behind his back and stepped forward with a small *ta-da*. "It seems I have become the main point of contact for the strange things people have been finding all over the place. Apparently dropped from the sky." He handed over the top hat to Glenmore.

"Well I never. It looks undamaged." Glenmore sat it on

his lap so that he could brush it with his good hand, then set it on top of his head.

"I reckon we might get the rest of the stuff back," said Tariq. "Eventually."

"Thank you so much, Tariq," said Penny. "For everything."

A thought occurred to Izzy. "How long would it take for you to forget what I looked like?" she asked Penny.

"What?"

She waved an impatient hand at Glenmore. "Glenmore rightly said we wouldn't expect people to forget what their scarecrows would look like after a day's absence, but..."

"What are you getting at?"

"Eve Bennefer, Ulrike Merrison and that Becky George were all police officers together, twelve plus years ago."

"Who are we talking about now?" said Glenmore.

"The woman who fell from the castle wall, and the woman who died in Pageant House," said Penny.

"Oh, a bad business that," said Nanna Lem. "That house is cursed."

Izzy gripped Penny's arm. "All three women were white and blonde and, let's say, of a type. We know Becky was watching Pageant House when Ulrike turns up. Aubrey assumed she was Eve Bennefer. What if Becky George did too?"

"They were friends."

"Colleagues. Maybe not close. What if, after she'd flung Aubrey out, Ulrike also comes outside. Superficially, she looks like the woman of the house."

"Ooh."

"And when Ulrike takes a walk up to the castle, maybe just playing the tourist, Becky follows her. They meet on the castle wall. Who knows what occurs between them, but there's an argument and Ulrike is pushed. It's a case of mistaken identity."

"*Top Hat*," Penny whispered. "So Becky killed Ulrike thinking it was Eve."

"Do you know what they're talking about?" Nanna Lem whispered to Glenmore.

"Not a clue, my dear," he replied.

"I find it's sometimes best just to nod and pretend to look interested," said Marcin. He put on a fixed grin and there was a look in his eyes that was manically over-attentive.

"That's the face you pull when I talk to you about sewing," Nanna Lem told Glenmore.

Glenmore put on the same the expression and nodded politely.

"Becky killing Ulrike makes sense," said Penny. "At least in terms of what then happened with the jacket and that. It doesn't explain how Becky got off the wall without being seen."

"Ah, well, that's where the scream comes in, I think," said Izzy.

"The scream?"

"Yes, it's too long. Come." She stood and turned to Nanna Lem and Glenmore. "Excuse us a minute. I need to show Penny something."

"You go ahead," said Nanna Lem. "Go talk nonsense."

Glenmore waved his assent with one hand and then reached for a fresh slice of Victoria sponge.

"Monty and I will show them our new trick," said Marcin, happily.

Izzy hurried Penny from the tent and was about to direct her attention to the castle wall when they bumped, almost quite literally, into Remi de Smet.

46

"Penny!" said Remi.

"Remi!" said Penny.

Penny was frozen. She didn't know what to say. She'd had to cancel one evening out with this Belgian fellow because of the scarecrow craziness. That was bad enough, but to sleep through like a hibernating bear on the second night. There was nothing to say but...

"I am so sorry."

"No. You? Why? It is me who must apologise a hundred times," he said.

"You must have come to the shop and I wasn't there."

"I'm usually so punctual," he said.

"Me too. But I was so tired and I didn't realise—"

"And then I got so caught up in the birdwatching because — Oh, it's no excuse but..." He produced his camera and tilted the screen towards her. A click and there was a brown-bodied bird in flight, its little yellow legs dangling behind it.

Penny frowned. "The, er, white-tailed lapwing?" she guessed.

"Yes! It was marvellous to see. She settled on the edge of the mere and I even got a chance to sketch her." He whipped out his sketch pad. Somehow the simple lines of the bird drawing gave the creature life that a crystal clear photograph could not.

"Lovely drawing," said Izzy.

"But I was too distracted," said Remi. "And I was late and you didn't come to the door when I finally did arrive at the shop and..." He sighed sadly.

Penny opened her mouth, preparing to say something that wasn't quite a lie but which skirted round the truth and made her seem generous and forgiving in the face of his poor timekeeping, then opted for the simple truth.

"I fell asleep," she said. "I slept right through, afternoon, evening, night. Even if you'd been on time..."

"You mean you were...?"

Penny put her hands to the side of her head as though sleeping and nodded.

A smirk appeared at the corner of Remi's mouth, expanding into a grin almost instantly. "Nothing is ever normal, is it?"

"No."

A hand grabbed Penny's arm and wheeled her sharply aside. She suddenly found herself hip to hip with Carmella Mountjoy.

"Well," Carmella purred. "This is most delicious, isn't it?"

"Er, afternoon, Carmella," said Penny.

Carmella flung out an expressive arm. "The scarecrow

festival proceeding as if nothing untoward had ever happened, and these gormless locals are none the wiser."

"I think some of them have perhaps noticed."

"You give them too much credit, Miss Slipper. I was wrong to think we should have covered up our mishap with a simple cleansing fire. What we did was something much bolder, more brilliant."

"Have you properly caught up with your sleep?" said Izzy.

Izzy was right. There was a buzzing manic wakefulness in Carmella's eyes, as though the lights were shining brightly but there was no one at home.

"I couldn't sleep at all," said Carmella. "The whole thing was just too exciting. And now we will see which of us will walk away with the star prize." She gestured to her husband Frank, who was deep in heated discussions with Stuart Dinktrout a short distance away. "I'm glad they're putting appropriate consideration into their final decision."

"They're the judges of the whole thing?" said Penny.

"The *key* judges," she said.

"I think all the scarecrows look lovely," said Remi.

Carmella scowled. "I think you're missing the whole point of a competition!" she snapped. Then her attention was drawn by someone across the way. "Hey, you! You're meant to look at the scarecrows, not touch them! That dress is from the original West End production, you know—!" She stalked off in order to remonstrate with the transgressor.

"She is ... wired," said Remi. "Yes?"

"She's a woman in need of sleep," Penny agreed. "I wonder if Stuart and Frank are seriously considering giving her the prize."

"I don't think they're considering anything of the sort," said Izzy, theatrically cocking a hand to her ear.

Penny tried to listen in. Stuart was waving his phone screen in front of Frank's face.

"See here, my man took the photo and you can clearly see Arabella over the finishing line."

"I can clearly see your man stood at an angle up the beach to make it look like she was more advanced," said Frank. "And yet Grenville is still very much about to cross the line first."

"There is the line – and what is there?"

"A shadow!" Frank fumed. "We were racing pigs, not pigs' shadows. But there, despite your attempts at trick photography, we see a portion of Grenville clearly about to cross the line first. To wit: his little pink snout."

"To wit?" said Stuart.

"To wit," Frank insisted.

"Bloody going off like a barn owl again. You do make the stupidest bloody utterances when you know you're in the wrong."

Remi approached the men, tapping Stuart on the shoulder as he did.

"What is it?" demanded Stuart furiously.

"I must, politely, correct your mistake," said Remi.

"What on earth are you on about?" said Frank.

"The barn owl. It does not go 'to wit'."

"What?"

"The female tawny owl makes a 'too-wit' sound, hoping for the male to answer 'too-woo'. The barn owl, if I may, makes more of..." Remi let loose with a discordant screeching sound that caused both of the pig fanciers to take a step back.

When he had done, the two men just stared in befuddlement. Remi gave them a little smile, an even littler bow, and backed away. The two men were still staring at him as Penny put her arm through his and escorted him away.

"That was magnificent," she told him, then turned to Izzy. "You were saying something about the scream...?"

"Yes," said Izzy. She waved a hand towards the stairs leading up to the top of the castle wall. "I'll show you."

"You appear to have lost Marcin somewhere."

"Entertaining Nanna Lem," she said dismissively. "There's cake so I'm sure he's happy."

47

"Why are we going up the stairs?" said Remi as they climbed the stone steps to the castle battlements.

"This is where, we think, Becky George pushed Ulrike Merrison to her death," said Penny.

"Becky who was staying with me?"

"The same," said Penny and filled him in on the salient details.

"So, two women are dead, killed by the third," he said, when they were at the top of the wall. "But why?"

"Casino cash," said Izzy.

"A bag of money?"

"I've been wondering about that," said Penny. "What if it was a lot of money? I mean *a lot*. Before I fell asleep in my armchair last night – yes, that's what I did – I was reading about the Hunterton Casino. Organised crime, fraud – it was all a bad deal. What if someone at some point had squirrelled away a ton of money?"

"How much?" said Izzy.

"Enough to buy Pageant House outright for one thing," Penny suggested.

Izzy mulled this over. "The casino burned down. In the act of rescuing the homeless man from the fire, they found this secret stash of money and— No, that doesn't feel right."

"Of course," said Penny. "It isn't right. Strike it, reverse it. What if… what *if*… You see, I didn't understand how it was that three police officers might be happening to pass a casino when it was burning down. Why wasn't the fire service there first?"

"There could be a number of reasons," said Remi.

"True, true. But were the police there because there was someone sleeping rough in the casino or were they just checking an abandoned building as part of their patrol? Something of that sort. And then, inside, or in a basement, or hidden somewhere, they found the huge wodge of cash."

"Wodge," said Remi. "A very English sounding word."

"They find it and decided to take it. To take it and to share it. A secret deal. Then, to cover their crime, they took the Carmella option: a nice cleansing fire."

"They burned down the casino to hide the evidence," said Izzy.

"Someone, possibly someone evil and nasty had put that money there, but if it was destroyed in a fire…"

"And the rough sleeper: that was only a cover story?"

"Or they only realised someone was in there after they started the fire," suggested Remi.

"Also possible," said Penny.

"They took the money to share it out," said Izzy. "But that doesn't explain why, years later, they all came here, unless..." She made a thoughtful hum. "Unless Eve Bennefer cheated them out of the money."

Penny liked that idea. "Eve stole all the money from her co-conspirators, quit the police, and has managed to keep a low profile for the last twelve years."

"Until the movement of a chest of drawers led to Monty finding a bag of money in the street and becoming a brief internet sensation. Enough for eagle-eyed Ulrike Merrison and Becky George to spot in the local news."

Remi nodded, but he was drawn to the vista looking out over the castle wall. "This is a beautiful view," he said, arms wide.

He was right. From here one looked out across the glistening mere, past the college grounds beyond, and over the houses and trees between the town and the village of Saxtead. The sun, hot though it might have been, brought a shimmering golden hue to everything.

"This is where Ulrike Merrison died," said Izzy, almost reluctantly, as though she did not want to ruin the moment. "I think Becky pushed her, probably initially thinking Ulrike was Eve. I don't suppose we'll ever know. She pushed her over the edge. Penny, do the scream."

Penny drew her head back, frowning.

"Do the scream," said Izzy.

Penny, feeling a mite embarrassed, did a little repeat of the scream in a constricted falsetto.

"That's pretty much what you did before," Izzy agreed.

She pointed over the edge. "The wall is less than ten metres high here. I used a thing on the internet called a splat calculator."

"A splat calculator? Really?" said Penny.

"It would take someone one and half seconds to fall that distance. Your scream was twice that long."

"I might have misjudged."

Izzy stuck out her bottom lip and tilted her head, appreciating the point. "Maybe, or maybe you heard a scream longer than one and a half seconds."

"How is that possible?"

"Did she start screaming before she fell?" said Remi.

Izzy put her hands on the wall. "What we know is that Ulrike was up here with someone – Remi's photo shows that – and that Ulrike fell to her death. You heard a scream, Penny, and came running. Moments later, Aubrey or Monica were stood here. There was no one around."

"That's correct."

"I learn new things every day. Only just now I learned that the twit-twoo sound owls make is two owls. You hear a thing and I guess you make the most obvious assumptions."

"The twit-twoo thing is linked to the scream?" said Penny.

"The point is, things don't have to be linked."

"Erm – and I'm seriously trying to following what's going on here – but what do you mean?"

"Picture this," said Izzy and pulled Penny towards the wall.

"I'm not going to be treated to a graphic demonstration, am I?"

48

"Don't worry," Izzy said. She turned Penny so she was facing over the wall towards the mere. "Becky and Ulrike were up here, talking, arguing, whatever. Remi takes his photo – click! – and moments later Becky pushes Ulrike off – but Ulrike doesn't scream. No one *has* to scream when they fall. She might not even have had time to draw breath."

"But I heard a scream."

"Ah-ha!" said Izzy. "So, now Becky is up here, Ulrike's corpse is down there and someone is likely to spot it soon. Probably some nosey shop-owner and her dog. But Becky knows there are other people in the castle grounds. If she walks out now, particularly at the moment the body is found, then she will be questioned and the jig will be up. So what does she do?"

"What does she do?" said Remi, fascinated.

"She goes down here," Izzy said and beckoned them to

follow her to the stairs. "I'm guessing Aubrey hadn't quite reached this point by then. He was here only minutes before the scream." Izzy followed the stairs for a while, then took the turning through the arch into the inner corridor partway up the wall. "She comes here."

She stopped at the window where she and Penny had unsuccessfully tried to squeeze themselves through. "She gets up on tippy-toes, or even climbs a little. She puts her mouth as close to the opening as possible and screams. Sadly for her, she screams a little too long."

"Wow," said Remi.

"Outside, Penny runs round to the body. Up above, Aubrey and Monica dash to see what has happened and finds the battlements conveniently empty. Becky has made it appear that Ulrike jumped to her death. When everyone then goes outside to help, Becky simply walks out the front gate of the castle and away."

"Disposing of her distinctive jacket among the things outside the charity shop in case anyone later remembers the 'Norfolk woman' in the colourful jacket who came into the castle earlier," added Penny.

"This is very clever," said Remi.

"At some point, she realises the woman she's killed is not Eve Bennefer," said Penny.

"So, she's still waiting for Eve to return," Izzy agreed.

"She stops spending her days in the ice cream parlour. It was too suspicious."

Izzy wagged a finger. "The little camera outside Pageant House! I bet it's one of them Bluetooth wireless ones and she was watching the door on her phone."

"The night of our meal out," Penny said to Remi, "she had her feet up by the fire pit but then left."

"The night we found Eve's body in the house," said Izzy. "Now that Eve had returned from her holiday, Becky went over and ... I guess history repeated itself. Except with the real Eve Bennefer."

"Becky George killed them both," Penny nodded. "All to get the money from the casino."

It suddenly felt a lot cooler in the dark corridor.

"We have to tell the police," said Izzy as they stepped away from the embrasure and walked down the steps to the inner keep once more.

"But it is all just speculation," said Penny.

"Yes. But it's right. It all fits."

Penny nodded, exhaling slowly. "You're right. We can phone Dennis Chang and tell him. Give him what we know about Becky George. We don't have a picture, do we?"

Remi struggled with his backpack. "I might... Wait a minute."

"You have a picture of her?"

At the bottom of the steps, he won his battle with the backpack and pulled out his sketchbook.

"You drew a picture?"

"I sketch a lot," he said. "I ask permission first."

He flicked through the thick cream pages of his pad. Images of birds and plants dominated. Some little more than dynamic line sketches, some more fully realised.

"Er, excuse me," said Penny, sticking her hand in to stop him at a page.

There were three separate sketches of Penny in different

sizes. In only one had she been drawn facing the viewer. In the others she was turned or looking aside, caught in innocent and unguarded moments.

"I ... I might have drawn a couple of sketches of you," he said, blushing.

"They're very flattering," said Penny.

"It's you," he said simply.

Izzy cleared her throat. "Becky George, if you wouldn't mind. She might be here, right now. It would be good to know what she looks like."

"Sure, sure," said Remi and turned back a few pages. "It's just a simple drawing but..."

He presented it to them. Penny was nodding in recognition but Izzy gripped the pad.

"No, that's not—"

"What?" said Penny.

Izzy looked around herself, almost frantic in her manner, then with an "Ah-ha!" took the pad and hurried off. Penny and Remi could only follow.

Aubrey and Dr Denise were stood inspecting a scarecrow with a makeshift surgical mask over the lower half of its face.

"It must be yours," Aubrey was saying in an unconvincing voice.

"That's not my old stethoscope. Or my gown. None of it is the same."

"Well, that just seems improbable," said Aubrey.

Izzy grabbed hold of him in her manic zeal and thrust the sketchbook under his nose.

"What's this?" he said, pulling back a little in order to focus properly.

"That woman," said Izzy. "Who is she?"

"It's a good drawing. Did you—?"

"Who is she?"

Aubrey blinked and then gave it a slow appraisal. "I've never met her but—"

"Look at her!"

"I am looking, Izzy, please."

"I don't know what's come over her," said Penny, apologetically. She was about to say it was Becky George, a woman possibly guilty of two murders, when Aubrey spoke again.

"It's the woman we saw in Pageant House," he said. "The dead one."

49

Six people and one dog walked down from the noisy scarecrow festival to Pageant House.

"What are we doing now?" Denise said to Marcin.

"I find it better not to ask," Marcin said. "There is madness in their method."

"You mean method in their madness."

Marcin tilted his head. "I like my version better."

"Is life always this exciting in the English countryside?" Remi asked.

"You have to make your own entertainment," Marcin said after much thought.

As they neared the house, and Aubrey became a little reluctant, Penny firmly held out her hand for him to give her the key.

He obliged and she opened the door into the kitchen.

"Are we all going in?" said Denise.

"You can if you like," said Penny. "We're just going to talk."

"To whom?"

She shrugged. "A ghost, I guess."

Izzy led the way inside. It was the third time she'd been inside the house this week, and for the first time she didn't feel any qualms. She had a grasp of the truth as her sword and armour and she strode through confidently.

"Upstairs?" she said to Penny.

"Upstairs, I think," Penny replied.

The two of them went up quickly, Aubrey and Remi followed at a distance.

"Hello!" Izzy called out. "Don't worry! It's just Izzy and Penny. We run the dressmaking shop in the town."

She reached the landing. There was no one there.

"We just wanted to come say hi," said Penny loudly. "All this week, both of us thought we'd met you or seen you, but we've only just realised our mistake."

Izzy turned around. Dust motes caught the sunlight streaming in from the big window above the stairs. It was the only movement in an otherwise lifeless house. Cursed or not, Izzy was acutely struck that this felt like a sad house.

"We know about the money from Hunterton's Casino," she said. "We think you and Ulrike and Becky found it all those years ago and hid it so that you might share it. We don't know if you started the fire deliberately. It must have been a shock though, to find there was someone still inside. But you saved him, after a fashion."

Penny put her hand on a packing case, still unopened after the move.

"But you took the money, kept it all for yourself, then laid low for the longest time before coming here and buying this house."

"Nice house," said Izzy. "Aubrey's done a bang up job with the decorating. Bit large for one person mind."

"We assume you didn't know that Becky had killed Ulrike on Monday. We think she mistook Ulrike for you, at least at first. And then when Becky turned up here the other night... She'd already killed one woman – she was probably prepared to kill another."

"A bit of natural justice for Becky maybe," said Izzy, looking at the polished banister over the stairs. "She pushed Ulrike off the castle and you... Did you mean to push her, or did she just fall in the struggle?"

"Anyway, we've told the police," said Penny. "It's up to them to sort it out, I guess. They'll want to hear your side of the story."

Izzy took a step towards the attic hatch.

"We kept saying to ourselves that old houses make noises," she said, her voice still raised. "Maybe even bats in the attic. We didn't think—"

She stopped. The wooden hatch was shifting. It was pulled aside and then an extending ladder gently unfolded.

The woman who descended did so on wobbly legs. Her unwashed blonde hair was pulled back in a rough ponytail. When she reached the bottom, she brushed loft dust off her T-shirt and turned to them. She still had a deep holiday tan and looked like she hadn't washed or slept in days.

"Hello," said Izzy in her kindest voice. "Eve Bennefer, I presume. It's very nice to meet you."

50

The police officers who turned up at Pageant House needed everything explaining to them twice. However, given that Eve was wanted for questioning by the police already, and the gang of individuals at the house were all too happy to provide the officers with their contact details, they were soon walking back up to castle together.

"I have never helped solve a murder before," said Remi.

"It would be hard to say how many crimes Eve, Becky and Ulrike had actually committed between them," said Penny.

"At least all that confusing and upsetting business is put to bed," said Denise, hugging Aubrey's arm close to her. And if Penny thought the gesture was a little patronising, as though Aubrey was a big stupid dog who had got himself into trouble, she kept such thoughts to herself.

There were the harsh sounds of a PA system being tested in the grounds of the castle.

"We haven't missed the scarecrow judging," said Marcin. "Quick!"

They moved briskly across the bridge over the moat and into the castle proper. Monica on the ticket table waved them through. The little money chest for taking entry fees had bank notes literally poking out of the sides. If the crowds here on this sunny day weren't enough to raise funds for the Community Change charity to buy a minibus for the older folks and scouts, then Penny would be very much surprised.

Ahead, on a low stage of wooden blocks, Stuart Dinktrout and Frank Mountjoy stood side by side. Very much the two men in their preferred element: raised above the common folk in a position of minor but certain power. Neither of them actually needed a microphone to be heard in any environment, but they had them nonetheless.

"It is time to announce the winners of the scarecrow competition," declared Frank. "It has been a very difficult process judging them all, but there was one clear winner."

"And we know who that is," said Carmella, appearing smoothly between Penny and Izzy.

"Whoever wins, it will be well-deserved," said Izzy.

"Thank you," said Carmella.

"The runners up—" Frank began, but Stuart cut across him.

"Excuse me, Frank, don't you have an announcement to make first?"

Frank looked at him, going somewhat pale, then nodded stiffly.

"Yes, just a small announcement. Yesterday, I had the

pleasure of racing my star pig Grenville against Mr Dintrout's little porker—"

"Arabella. Her's name Arabella," interjected Stuart with a curious blend of annoyance and pride.

"Yes," said Frank. "An *unofficial* race along the sands at Great Yarmouth in which Arabella was indeed the faster pig."

"Queen of pigs!" crowed Stuart, beaming the biggest smile Penny had ever seen on his usually controlled face.

"That's a big admission," said Penny.

"Ah, wait," said Izzy softly. "No, I see what's going on."

"You do?"

"The runners up," continued Frank. "In third place, we have Finding Nemo—" there was polite and scattered applause "—and in second place is Freddie Mongrelly." More applause followed.

"Here it comes," said Izzy.

"But the winner—" said Frank, with mounting volume and pleasure, "—is Elphaba from *Wicked*!"

Carmella squealed like an over-excited schoolgirl and clapped along with everyone else as she rushed towards the stairs.

Penny narrowed her eyes. "Hang on..."

"Yep," said Izzy. "Frank concedes the pig race to Stuart, and miraculously the two of them agree to let Frank's wife have the big prize."

"What a town we live in," said Penny, but the two of them clapped along anyway. The sun was up, the people of the town were joined in celebration, and there was little that could dampen the happy mood.

"What's the prize? What's the prize?" Carmella said, giving her husband the briefest of kisses on the cheek before turning round in anticipation.

Stuart put his microphone to his mouth. "First prize, courtesy of our good friends at Suffolk Blimps, is a day's ride in a hot air balloon!"

There was more clapping.

"That would have been nice," pouted Izzy. "Can you imagine?"

"I think Carmella can imagine," said Penny. "Can't get more than a dozen feet off the ground, I believe."

On the stage, Carmella looked panicked, almost terrified, as though she was about to be whisked into the sky at that very moment.

"Ah – the biliousness," said Izzy.

"It's a medical condition, I believe," said Penny.

There was frantic conferring on the stage.

"She does not seem very happy with her prize, no?" said Remi, close to Penny.

"Some people are never happy," she replied.

After some awkwardness on stage, Frank spoke. "Mrs Mountjoy has, um, very kindly decided that she does not need such a generous gift. Perhaps there's another prize...?" He looked hopefully to Stuart.

"Nope," said Stuart, very happy about the fact. "Are we awarding the balloon ride to second place?"

Frank sighed and shrugged.

"Very well!" said Stuart. "Then the first place prize—"

"Only the prize, not first place itself!" said Frank.

"—The first place *prize* goes to Freddie Mongrelly!"

There was more applause, although the enthusiasm had died a little since the crowd had already done plenty of clapping by now.

Marcin walked forward and stepped up onto the stage.

"Marcin?" said Izzy.

Marcin shook hands first with Stuart and then Frank.

"Did you know that was his scarecrow?" said Penny.

"I knew nothing of the sort. That man is full of surprises," said Izzy.

Marcin took the small voucher from Stuart and held it aloft like it was the biggest trophy in the world. His eyes sought out Izzy in the crowd and gave her a knowing and loving smile. She whistled loudly and clapped all the harder.

"A fine prize," said Remi.

Penny looked down and took hold of his hand.

"Sometimes we're just lucky," she said.

ABOUT THE AUTHOR

Millie Ravensworth writes the Cozy Craft series of books. Her love of murder mysteries and passion for dressmaking made her want to write books full of quirky characters and unbelievable murders.

Millie lives in central England where children and pets are something of a distraction from the serious business of writing, although dog walking is always a good time to plot the next book

ALSO BY MILLIE RAVENSWORTH

Death at Westminster (in collaboration with Rachel McLean)

Diana Bakewell is London's savviest and best connected tour guide.

As the lead guide at Chartwell and Crouch Tours, she's busy teaching her young assistant Zaf the ropes alongside dealing with company politics and her slimy boss. In her spare time she's helping Zaf find his feet in London and coming to terms with the fact that a tabby cat called Gus has stowed away on her vintage tour bus.

But when Diana and Zaf take a group of students on a tour of the Houses of Parliament and an MP's researcher dies, Diana suspects all is not as it seems.

The police are at a loss. They interview witnesses, including Diana's tour group, but seem to be getting nowhere. Diana, however, was at the scene. She witnessed people's reactions when the young woman died and knows that there's a link between her group and the murder.

Can Diana solve the crime and ensure justice is done, while keeping her tour group under control around London and protecting Chartwell and Crouch Tours' reputation?

Death in Westminster is the first part in a playful cozy mystery series set in a nostalgic version of London. Perfect for fans of Richard Osman, Anthony Horowitz and the Paddington books.

Death at Westminster

Printed in Great Britain
by Amazon